GHOST HUNTER'S DAUGHTER

DON'T MISS ANY OF
DAN POBLOCKI'S SPOOKY STORIES!

Shadow House

The Ghost of Graylock

The Haunting of Gabriel Ashe

The Book of Bad Things

The House on Stone's Throw Island

GHOST HUNTER'S DAUGHTER

DAN POBLOCKI

Scholastic Press
New York

Library of Congress Cataloging-in-Publication Data Available

ISBN 978-0-545-83004-1

10 9 8 7 6 5 4 3 2 1   20 21 22 23 24
Printed in the U.S.A.   23

First edition, July 2020
Book design by Keirsten Geise

This book is dedicated to my mother, Gail Roe, and to the memory of my grandmother, Doris Piehler, two of the strongest women in my life.

PART ONE

THE KNOCKING

Chapter One

CLAIRE FELT SOMEONE watching. As she approached her locker, a sensation came like the cool spring breeze that had snuck in through her open window earlier that morning, creeping through her blanket, seeping into her skin, and chilling her bones. She turned away from the lock and glanced down the half-empty hallway of Archer's Mills Middle School.

A boy was standing at the far end of the hall, clutching one strap of his ratty-looking backpack, his gaze like two lasers aimed at her face. It was enough to make Claire gasp.

His name came to her.

Lucas Kent.

Though they'd been in several classes together, Claire did not know the boy well. She stared back. Lucas flinched when her eyes met his, then moved quickly down the stairs behind him.

Claire shuddered. She fiddled with the lock hanging from her locker, spinning the numbers again and again, as if that would make the chilly feeling go away.

A finger poked at her spine.

Claire startled, then turned to find her friend Norma Gillhop standing a little too close. "Gosh, I didn't mean to make you jump out of your jeans, Ghosty."

"No prob, Norma-l." Claire caught her breath and popped open her lock.

She told Norma about the boy who'd been staring.

"Lucas Kent? The creep! Do you want me to walk with you to your first class?"

"I'll be fine. Lucas doesn't scare me."

"His *grandmother* scares me. She's totally a witch."

Claire thought that kind of talk was cruel, so she

ignored it and shoved her bag into her locker, slamming the door shut.

"The group is meeting after school today, right?" Norma asked.

Claire nodded even though she wasn't sure she wanted to meet up with her ghost-story group today. Seeing Lucas Kent watching her had left a bad taste in her brain. The first bell chimed.

She caught Lucas staring again in the library a couple of hours later. Claire had just come around the end of one aisle when she discovered him peering through the library door at her. They locked glances for a moment before he took off again, bolting from view. She backed into the shadows between the shelves, trying to shrink down, her lungs fighting for breath.

Was he looking for her? If so, why did he keep running away?

What was it about him that was so unsettling?

When she mentioned Lucas's disappearing routine to her other friends in the cafeteria at lunch, Francine

Perkins burst out laughing. "Aww, Kent has a crush on the ghost hunter's daughter!"

Claire cringed. Lucas shared the same lunch period. What if he'd overheard Francine's outburst?

Claire didn't like upsetting anyone.

She also didn't like being called the ghost hunter's daughter, even though everyone in town, in the whole country, and even some parts of the world, knew it was the truth. Or *a* truth. Part of a truth anyway. It was true that her father hunted ghosts. But the other part of the truth was that Claire imagined herself as her own person, not just someone's daughter.

She knew that who she was on her own wasn't as impressive as being the ghost hunter's daughter. As a person, Claire Holiday was a girl with knees like doorknobs. Her Coke-bottle lenses made her eyes look twice as big as they actually were, and they were already pretty big. Her brown hair wilted like corn silk far below her shoulders, but it shone copper in the sun, so she didn't mind. Her socks often did not match. She was a voracious fan of science fiction paperbacks as well as a user of words like *voracious*.

The third encounter with Lucas was at the water fountain, right before the end of the day. Claire experienced that similar spring breeze sensation in her bones. She spun to find him standing several steps away.

Was Lucas waiting for a drink?

Again, their eyes met, but this time, Claire felt something pass between them. Something strange. Something she didn't have a word for. His lips parted as if he wished to speak. Then he reached around her for the fountain's button. "Excuse me," he whispered.

Flustered, Claire sidestepped far away from him. He leaned over the fountain. Cold water rushed down the drain.

After school, Claire walked with Norma and Francine, and their friends Mikey and Whit, through the woods behind the middle school, over the creek, to the nearby housing development where many of their classmates lived.

"Where are you taking us, Francine?" Claire asked.

"You don't already know?" Francine answered mysteriously.

Claire had a good idea, but she didn't like the direction they were heading.

The houses there had been built on what used to be an old farm. Now several detention basins protected the neighborhood from flooding. When the basins were dry, they looked like large empty ponds, and in the summer their grounds were covered in lush green lawns. But sometimes they filled up during storms and became like small lakes. At one side of each basin was a compact concrete opening connected to tunnels that passed into spillways at the creek by the school.

On this day, the sun was shining, the ground was dry, and the closest tunnel was waiting for the group to huddle inside. Dead leaves crunched beneath their sneakers, and their voices reverberated as they stepped into the shadows. Claire swallowed down her fear.

"I hope the ghost isn't hungry," said Whit. "I don't want to get eaten."

"I'm hungry," said Mikey. "Maybe I'll eat the ghost!"

"I brought snacks," said Norma. "How about you eat these instead? Cashews and yogurt chips."

"Yogurt chips?" Mikey whined. "But I'm lactose intolerant! Why not chocolate chips?"

"Next time bring your own," Francine said with a sneer.

Claire held out her hands, allowing her fingers to drag lightly against the gritty concrete walls. Cool light filtered in through the spillway entry behind her, casting her shadow forward along the path she was walking. There was a smell down here that was both dirty and clean at the same time—earth and minerals and the decay of washed-up leaves and twigs and the tiny bones of rodents that had drowned long ago.

"I brought this," said Whit, opening his backpack and sliding out his sparkly black-and-silver luchador mask.

"Who are you planning on wrestling?" asked Norma.

"No one." He slipped it over his head. "It makes me feel safe." Whit suddenly looked like a walking and talking sugar skull skeleton. "Sometimes the stories are a little too scary."

"Nobody forces you to come with us," said Francine, spreading out her jacket and sitting delicately on the tunnel floor. The others joined her, forming a small circle.

Whit clasped Mikey's hand. "Mikey asked me. And as long as he asks, I'll be here." His voice was muffled inside the mask.

Claire glanced into the shadowy part of the tunnel and shivered. Some of the kids from school had told stories of a boy who'd been swept away during a thunderstorm. They said that his ghost wandered these tunnels, looking for a way out.

As soon as Francine had gotten wind of the story, she insisted that they come find him.

"Let's just do this the way your father does it on television," Francine told Claire.

One of the ways that Miles was able to call forth the spirits on his show was to lie about them. To tell outrageous stories about their lives that would anger the spirits and make them appear. And once they appeared, Miles would use his special tools to capture them and send them away. Claire hated this. It felt mean, like a kid in high school picking on a defenseless third grader. So, she sat back and allowed her friends to tell the lies instead.

Francine began. "Hello? We know that you drowned here. You were our age. A boy whose name was . . . Argyle Mesnerfloof." The others snickered at the outrageous name that Francine had offered.

Norma added, "You came down here looking for something you lost. It was a . . . a golden football."

Mikey laughed and then leaned forward. "You used it to stare into as you brushed your teeth every night. But your sister threw it out the window. And it splashed down into the gutter and went through the grate at the curb. And that's why you ended up in these tunnels. You were looking for your football!"

"I love it!" Whit cheered.

A crunching of leaves resounded down the concrete tube, and the light in the passage went dim.

A silhouette was standing at the far end of the tunnel, near the spillway.

Goose bumps tickled Claire's scalp.

"Who's there?" she asked. When the figure didn't answer, Claire was struck with a sudden fear. They *had* angered the drowned boy. He was coming to make them pay for their lies. What would be the cost? The only escape route was the opposite direction, into the darkness of the detention tunnels. The silhouette came closer and Claire stood up, moving between it and the others. "Not one more step," she said, her voice wobbling.

Her echo mocked her, revealing her nerves to everyone, over and over.

A boy's voice called back. "Claire? Is that you?"

The silhouette lost its mystery. But it maintained its menace.

"It's Lucas." The voice was soft. "I . . . I need to talk to you."

Norma whispered into Claire's ear. "Should I tell him to shove off?"

"Talk to me about what?" Claire said, huddling closer to her friends.

"Your dad," Lucas answered. The day's events clicked into place.

Right, thought Claire. My dad. Everyone always wants to talk about my dad. Lucas was just another *fan*.

"Have you heard from him?" he asked.

Strange. This was not a usual fan's question.

Coldness emanated out of the tunnel walls, and the tips of Claire's fingers went numb where she held them against the concrete. "Not since he left town a couple of days ago," she answered hesitantly. "Why do you want to know?"

Lucas stepped closer. "I'm sorry, Claire, but wherever your father's at, he's in real trouble." A drip of water echoed out of the murk. Claire imagined the drowned boy wandering the tunnels, shuffling closer, milky eyes scanning the darkness for daylight. Lucas went on, "The kind of trouble someone doesn't come back from."

Chapter Two

Seven Days Ago

A WEEK BEFORE he followed Claire to the spillway behind the school, Lucas Kent had woken to the sound of knocking. It started slowly, uncertain and quiet, before growing louder.

Lucas sat up and clutched the blankets to his chin. He checked the clock. It was well past midnight. He wasn't sure he wanted to know who would be knocking so late, so he pressed his body against his mattress. Soon a desperate pounding was rattling his grandmother's house.

Gramma Irene's bedroom door sighed open. Sleepy footfalls shuffled to the staircase. *Creak, crick, creak.* She made her way to the foyer, mumbling something that Lucas couldn't make out.

He eased out of bed and hurried to the top of the stairs, careful to not make a sound, and then peered across the landing. His grandmother stood before the open front door. Cold night air rustled her white flannel nightgown. It was early spring, but the chill of winter still clung to the breeze. She was whispering to someone out there—it was too dark for Lucas to see. She didn't seem worried, but should *he* be? A rushing sound answered back, soft and low, like wind through trees.

When his grandmother closed the door and turned to the staircase, her face was hidden in shadow. Lucas rushed back to his room and slid under his covers. Seconds later, his bedroom door swung open. He could hear her breath as she stared in at him. He held still, not wanting her to know that he was awake.

Lucas loved his grandmother. He was also in awe of her.

Everyone in Archer's Mills knew that Irene Kent could speak to the dead.

For the rest of the night, his racing heart and flustered mind kept him at the edge of sleep, and he tossed and turned until early sunlight dared to peek through the curtains.

During breakfast, Irene glanced at him from across the table but said nothing. Silence throbbed like a drum in Lucas's head. When he couldn't take it anymore, he blurted out, "Who was at the door last night?"

Irene froze, her spoon halfway to her mouth. "So, you *did* hear," she answered. The corners of her eyes crinkled knowingly. He nodded. Irene folded her hands and squinted at him. "It was a man named Otto," she said. Gently, she added, "He wanted me to give a message to his wife."

Lucas squinted back, trying to match her expression. "Who's his wife? What's the message?"

"I haven't met Laura yet. He said that she'll be coming to the salon soon. He wanted me to tell her that her mother's ring is in a white box on a shelf at the back of her pantry. She's been looking for it for ages."

Lucas thought about this. "Otto was a—a *ghost*," he stated, struggling to keep his voice steady.

"A spirit," she answered, leaning back in her chair, folding her thin arms across her chest, covering the Harley-Davidson emblem on her gray T-shirt. "Yes. He was."

A funny feeling overtook Lucas. He wanted to get up from the table and run away. He wanted nothing to do with his grandmother's spirits. But curiosity sometimes weighs more than fear. He scooted his chair forward and took several quick bites of his cereal. Sugary marshmallows squeaked between his teeth.

Irene went on, her voice gentle, cautious. "You've always wanted to know how it works, Lucas. Now you do."

He thought about that. A bubble rose up through the milk and popped. "The spirits come at night?"

"Not every time. But they do always come with a knock. That's how our family has heard them for generations. My mother. Her grandfather. Back and back and back. Someone knocks. We answer." Irene reached across the table, silently asking for Lucas's hand. "And now it's happening to you."

Lucas didn't reach back. Irene forced a smile, tapped the table with her fingers, and then drew her hand into her lap. "I was a little older than you the first time I heard it," she said. "Don't worry. It only seems scary for a short time."

"What if . . . I don't answer?"

Irene scowled. "It's our duty to help people. Don't take this lightly, Lucas. You have a gift."

He thought of the knocking sound—how it had rattled the house. He thought of the whispering—how it had sounded like a voice, but also *not a voice*. "What if I don't want the gift?" Lucas asked.

"Bring it back to the store for a refund," Irene said without a bit of humor. She stood and whisked her bowl over to the sink. "Go on now," she said, her back to Lucas. "The school bus will be coming soon."

Lucas Kent had lived with Irene for the past two years. His mother and father worked along the coast for most of the year, in the zones that had been destroyed by the waves. They oversaw the rebuilding of the communities that had lost everything so that people could return to their homes in the emptied cities. His family decided that Lucas would be better off if he were settled in one place, so Lucas lived in his father's former bedroom for now. The old wallpaper made him smile. He imagined his father at his age, falling asleep every night, staring at the same illustrations of astronauts and rocket ships blasting fire into an indigo expanse.

When he'd first arrived at Archer's Mills Middle School, Lucas had a hard time fitting in. On one of his first days, during lunch, a girl named Francine had observed that one of his eyes seemed to be higher up on his face than the other.

"So, you're kind of deformed, right?" she'd asked.

"You're not so perfect yourself," he'd answered.

Other kids had laughed, but after that, no one wanted him to sit at their table. Francine had made sure of it.

Lucas missed his friends in his old town. Once, he'd walked to the bus stop near the pharmacy and headed back all by himself. On the bus, he'd sat near a family with several children, trying to blend in with them when the driver had collected tickets.

When Irene had learned what he'd done, she'd been furious, but it was the disappointment in her eyes that had kept him from hopping the bus again.

The morning after he'd heard the knocking, Lucas had risen early.

The day passed in a haze. Lucas had paid little attention during classes. He'd picked at the crusts of his peanut butter and jelly sandwich at lunch, not eating any of it. He'd kept thinking about the man—*the spirit*—named Otto whom his grandmother had met at the front door, about the message Gramma was supposed to give to the man's wife at the salon. He'd wondered how often she had been wakened by knocking that he'd never heard—how many times since she'd been about his age, when her gift had begun to develop. How often would it happen to him now that he'd started hearing it too? If he'd gotten to the door first, would Otto have given the message to *him* instead?

In the cafeteria, a group of girls who were sitting a few tables away glanced at him and giggled. He recognized Francine and some of her friends. One of them, a dark-haired girl named Claire, locked eyes with him for a moment before looking quickly away. A prickly sensation shot up his neck.

She was the ghost hunter's daughter.

Claire had moved to Archer's Mills only a few years before Lucas. But her experience had been the opposite of his own. Her father, Miles Holiday, was the host of a popular television show that documented ghosts and the supernatural. Lucas made sure to watch every episode, like most of the kids at Archer's Mills Middle School. Having a famous father made Claire famous too. It was rare to observe her unaccompanied by a crew of fawning friends. The odd thing was that she didn't seem to want the attention. She always looked slightly miserable when they all offered to be her partner for a class project or begged for a tale of ghostly intrigue.

Whenever Lucas put on *Invisible Intelligence*, Miles Holiday's TV show, his grandmother would fidget and fret, arguing with the screen, calling Miles a *Johnny-come-lately*, an *inexperienced charlatan* who used force and belligerence to send away lingering souls using *little empathy* and *zero finesse*.

Irene said that spirits are like children on the first day of kindergarten—you need to let them know what to expect, or else they'll be running the class.

At school, Lucas had once felt bold enough to share his grandmother's opinion of Miles. Afterward, tales spread like toxic gas that Lucas had called Claire's dad a fool, a jerk, a fake. Those weren't even the words he had used. For a long time, everyone would glare at him, and one day, an older boy even swatted his books from his hands, scattering them down the hallway like a trail of slime left by a slug.

Such was the unwitting power of the girl they called the ghost hunter's daughter.

On the day after he'd heard the knocking, he turned away from the giggling girls in the cafeteria, crumpled up what was left of his lunch, and tossed it all in the garbage.

A few days after that, at a moment just after twilight, Lucas was curled up on the couch in the living room, flipping through the television channel guide, when the porch steps creaked outside.

Lucas's grandmother owned the hair salon on Beech Nut Street. Several nights a week, she took late appointments. Lucas would come home after school, do his homework, then heat up a microwave meal and watch television, waiting for her to return.

Apparently, Gramma was home earlier than usual.

In the back of his mind, Lucas expected to hear the rattle of her keys and the click of the lock, but the noise didn't come. He glanced toward the foyer.

The window in the door was covered in a gauzy curtain. A figure stood on the other side, its silhouette backlit by the streetlight at the end of the long driveway.

"Gramma?" he called out. "Did you forget your key?"

No answer came.

Lucas squirmed backward, pressing his body into the space between the couch cushions.

The tapping began softly.

He didn't feel ready for this to happen to him again so soon.

He shook his head. He closed his eyes.

The tapping grew louder. It did not stop.

Lucas sprinted to the hallway, slipped into the coat closet, and then closed the slatted wood door behind him. The knocking turned to pounding. He squeezed his eyes shut again, his stomach churning with terror.

The front door's knob rattled and squeaked as it turned. Hinges squealed. Lucas held his breath.

Cold air crept into the house, slipping under the closet door and nipping at Lucas's ankles. He leaned against the wall. His grandmother's leather jackets enveloped him, blocking out the light from the hall. There was a change in the air, a pressure that clogged his ears.

Even though he'd heard the front door open, the tapping went on.

A loud voice called out from the living room, where he'd been sitting moments earlier. Lucas nearly screamed.

But he knew that voice. It was as familiar to him as his grandmother's. *Tonight, we'll look back at some of our favorite locations,* said the voice, *to see how they have transformed since our last visit.* It was Miles Holiday, speaking from the television. The ghost hunter himself. *These towns have become popular spots on the recent map of our changing country,* Miles went on. *In some cases, growing crowds make pilgrimages, seeking answers to—*

Whoever had entered the house had turned on the show that Claire Holiday's father hosted, *Invisible Intelligence.*

The volume jolted up to an almost painful level. Lucas clapped his hands to his ears. Someone was trying to draw him out of his hiding place.

As the voice went on, loudly, Lucas strained to hear another sound underneath it. Footsteps. Breath . . . Anything that might give away the intruder's location in the house.

The tapping grew louder. Now it was a knocking— knuckles hitting hard against some unseen surface.

If I time it right, Lucas thought, I might escape.

Judging from the cold air at his ankles, the front door was still open. He could run outside and down the steps—

The closet door shook. Lucas brought his hand to his mouth and clamped it tightly against his skin. The knocking became a hammering. The wooden panels rattled as if about to break. Any moment, clawlike fingers would reach through and—

Lucas crouched, feeling for something heavy to use as a weapon. His grandmother's black umbrella? Good enough ... He stood and then braced himself, raising the sharp point of the umbrella over his head. The hammering intensified. He hooked the umbrella onto his elbow and pressed his fists to his ears, which made him realize that most of the din was inside his own head.

"What do you want!?" he shrieked.

The noise kept up, transforming into an impossible noise that seemed to be made of wind and machinery and fire. His heart galloped in his chest. There was only one thing he knew would stop it.

He opened the door.

Everything paused. The commotion. The pressure. The voice from the television.

All his panic was wiped away, and now he could only stare with wonder.

Standing before him was a woman Lucas didn't recognize. Her face seemed to shimmer and change in the way faces in dreams can shift and blur. Lucas couldn't tell if the woman was tall or short, if her skin was dark or light, if her expression was angry or calm. Her body was edged with silver, reflecting an otherworldly glow that seemed to be cast from nowhere.

"Who are you?" Lucas managed to ask.

Her voice echoed from somewhere above or below, right behind him or maybe far away. *Help me*, she said. Those weren't quite the words she'd used, but their meaning came through to him as clear as a windowpane. Wavering emotions rode along with it. Hope and awe and fear . . .

And fear

And *fear* . . .

The longer he stayed quiet, the more her panic grew.

Like a force of nature, it thrummed and thrashed, trying to breach his mind. Lucas straightened his spine, forcing himself to stand still. He thought back to the conversation he'd had with his grandmother. *It only seems scary for a short time*, she'd said.

How short a time?

He'd never felt this frightened, and not only because of this woman, the one who'd knocked, but because of what it meant for the future. *His* future.

Was this how it would be?

"I think you're looking for my grandmother," he said steadily. "She's the one who—"

The woman held up a hand, and Lucas's voice dried up in his mouth.

No, child, she said. *I've come for you.*

Chapter Three

Now

"I'M SORRY, CLAIRE," said Lucas, "but wherever your father's at, he's in real trouble. The kind of trouble someone doesn't come back from."

Claire felt warmth drain away from her face. Norma slipped her cool fingers between Claire's. Her friends stood up beside her.

"No one invited you, Kent," said Francine.

Lucas was still for a few seconds. "I know this isn't something you want to hear, Claire, but you've got to trust me."

"Trust you?" Claire heard herself say. The seed of a

storm was spinning in her chest. "I don't even know you, Lucas."

"That's true." Lucas swallowed hard. "You don't. Not many kids in this town do." He was still a dozen yards away, his face hidden in shadow. "I'm sorry I spooked you at school today. I needed to tell you, but . . . I didn't know how."

"So, you followed us here instead," said Whit, pulling off the luchador mask. His hair stood up, mussed. Mikey reached out and smoothed it down.

"How are you so sure Claire's dad is in trouble?" asked Norma. "Did your creepy grandmother tell you?" Claire squeezed Norma's hand to shush her.

"It wasn't my grandmother's message to share. I didn't even tell *her* what I know." Lucas's voice was the rustling of leaves through the tunnel, the breeze wheezing through the eaves of Claire's house, the pipes knocking in the basement whenever the heat kicked on. "A woman came to *me* this time. She said . . . she said she was your mother."

Mother.

Claire's skin turned to stone. Some of her organs too. Lungs. Liver. Spleen. Her heart worked harder to keep her blood pumping through places it didn't want to flow.

Francine cackled. "Nice try, Kent. Run along home now. Tell Granny the joke didn't work."

"I'm not joking. I would never"—his breath hitched—"*never* joke about something like this."

Claire's answer came out like a chirp. "You really spoke with my mother?"

Did she actually believe him?

Whit shoved himself through the group. "Leave us alone, Lucas," he growled. Mikey reached out and grabbed his wrist, pulling him back.

"Okay, okay," Lucas said, holding his hands up—a pair of white flags, surrendering. "I'll go. I didn't mean to scare anyone. I just wanted to . . . do my duty."

"Well, your duty is done," Mikey said. "Bye!"

Just before Lucas reached the end of the tunnel, he paused and then turned back. "You're going to need my help, Claire," he said sadly. "I'm sorry." He stepped out into the sunlight. The glare of the afternoon devoured his silhouette, and he was gone.

Silence echoed like a bell.

Claire wanted to believe he was being his usual strange self. He had bashed her father before, but what he'd said just now hadn't sounded cruel. Mostly just . . . honest.

Norma spoke up. "Are you okay, Claire?"

Claire's head felt heavy; she worried that if she nodded, it might topple off her neck.

"He's being a jerk again," said Mikey.

Whit slipped the mask over his head, hiding the crease that was running up his forehead.

"Let's get back to hunting ghosts," said Francine, trying to change the subject to one that was more to her liking. "That dead kid must still be down here some-where. Can we try raising him again?"

"I—I think I should go home," Claire answered. "I want to check on a few things."

"You don't really believe him, do you?" Norma asked

quietly. "Lucas basically admitted he was trying to freak you out all day long."

"That's not what—" Claire gave her friends a hard look. "Wouldn't *you* be freaked out?" They clamped their mouths shut. They weren't used to her responding harshly, even though she'd barely spoken above a whisper. "You know what people say about his grandmother. She *knows* things. Wouldn't it make sense that Lucas would have the same . . . ability?"

"But they also say his grandmother hates your father," answered Norma. "Maybe she put Lucas up to this."

Claire collected her belongings. Lucas's words were creeping into tiny crevices in her mind, tendrils grabbing hold.

"Do you want us to walk you home?" asked Whit.

"I'm a big girl." Claire brushed soil off her pants. "But thank you." She smiled her gap-toothed grin and then loped toward the end of the tunnel, leaving the others in the dark.

Chapter Four

CLAIRE WALKED UP and over the green hills, then down through the empty basins through the backyards of her neighbors.

All the while, her mind churned.

The idea that her mother's spirit had visited a possibly psychic boy in Claire's school made her heartbeat stumble. It was that old fear come true—her mother was still out there, wandering the world. Someone like her father could hunt down her spirit and send her away if he believed her to be too frightening, too threatening to people.

Years earlier, after the East Coast tsunami, there

were some who took comfort in believing that spirits lingered. They thought that the dead would pass along messages and memories, words of encouragement and of warning, to *sensitive* people. People like Irene Kent. Then there were others who believed that the dead's noisy voices might overwhelm the survivors and cause them to stumble on their life's path, that looking forward was always better than glancing backward.

Claire thought of Lucas's grandmother. Her father had once considered working with her on his television show. Irene was meant to have appeared occasionally as a ghostly expert. But something happened. A disagreement.

Miles wished to send the dead away.

Irene did not.

The Holidays' house appeared across the lawns, its red Victorian turret rising over barren branches. Spring was on its way, and evidence was all around. The neighborhood trees were still bare, yet green stalks rose from the earth near Claire's trail. The earliest flowers showed purple and white buds teasing with color. The Holidays' house was different from the others that surrounded it—older, opulent. The outside was decorated with details that Claire remembered her mother saying belonged to the Queen Anne style. There were oval windows made of stained glass. Its porches and porticoes were all curving lines, latticework, and pink-painted trim.

Claire adored living here. Her mother had picked out the house herself, imagining space enough for a large family that she and Miles had never managed to have. When she was little, Claire's parents had told her they'd taken that extra love and given it to her instead.

Before Penelope had gotten sick, the joyful design of the house had mirrored the family's life inside it. Claire remembered music and spontaneous dancing after delicious dinners, climbs to the top of the turret to spy on the neighbors from behind the compact, jewel-colored windows, and bicycle rides around the enormous basement on stormy days.

Silence can sound like thunder when it comes all of a sudden.

Penelope's illness arrived in the same way.

Her mother was gone before Claire even had a chance

to learn much about the monstrous thing that consumed her.

After it was over, late at night, Claire used to try talking to her. She'd ask if she was feeling better now that she was no longer inside her body. And if there were dogs and cats in heaven. And if she was still able to bake their favorite brownies. But Claire never got an answer—certainly nothing as solid as a knock on the front door of the red Victorian in the middle of the night.

As Claire climbed the wooden steps to the back porch, anger flash-banged through her skull. Had her mother really spoken to a boy she barely knew rather than to her own daughter? Claire threw open the kitchen door and stomped toward her father's office at the front of the house.

"Claire? Is that you, honey?" Aunt Lizzie was upstairs. "I was worried!"

"Sorry, Aunt Lizzie! I was with some friends."

"Please phone next time. I hate thinking of you lying in a ditch on the side of the road!"

Aunt Lizzie could be very dramatic, which was why

Claire had already decided to keep what Lucas had said a secret. She paused at the bottom of the great curving staircase. "Did Dad call in yet?"

"I haven't heard anything. He must be busy!"

Claire's cheeks burned red like a poisoned apple in a fairy tale.

Chapter Five

THE HINGES OF Miles's office door squeaked faintly. The scent of leather and pine tingled Claire's brain, bringing her father's face to the front of her imagination. His pointy nose. His trim brown beard. His hazel eyes, sparkling with wonder. The room was filled with the essence of him.

Whenever Claire was feeling sad, she would search the house for items that had once belonged to her mother—dresses that had been packed away in boxes, cartons of unsharpened pencils, Penelope's old pillow—and hold them to her nose, inhaling deeply. The smell of her mother was still so strong, it felt in those moments as if she were right there with Claire. She wondered if ghosts were merely memories provided by our senses— the five known ones, and possibly, a mysterious sixth.

Claire swung her backpack off her shoulders and rested it on a wooden chair by the window, then zipped it open. She removed her notebook and placed it on her father's desk. Sitting in his cushy swivel chair, she scanned the information she'd copied from his records: *Hush Falls Holler*; *ghost of Lemuel Hush*; *town at the bottom of the lake*; *Graveyard Watch* . . . She'd written all of it down while her father had been sleeping, before he'd left for this job. But Miles had taken his notebooks and maps with him on the trip, and all Claire was left with now were her own notes and a few scraps that littered the wide cherry surface of his workspace.

There had to be some way to reach him. Once, everyone had carried a cell phone, but the waves had knocked down so many towers on the East Coast that they'd made the devices nearly impossible to use anymore, at least around here. She flipped through her scrawl, searching for the name of his motel. But if he'd listed it, she'd neglected to copy it, and now she couldn't remember it. Maybe Aunt Lizzie knew the answer. But if Claire were to ask, Aunt Lizzie might insist that she was overly tired and then send her to bed early.

Instead, Claire picked up the phone and dialed Information. When an operator answered, Claire asked for the names and numbers of all the hotels or motels within several miles of Hush Falls. To her surprise, the operator provided only one: *Lost Village Motor Lodge.* Claire wrote the name and number in her book. "Can you connect me?" she asked the operator.

"Hold, please."

A tone pulsed from the earpiece for a few seconds before a gruff voice answered, "Motel!"

"Hello," said Claire. "I'm wondering if you have a guest staying with you named Miles Holiday?"

"Who wants to know?" asked the man on the other end.

"His daughter. Is he there?"

There was a pause, and then, "Checked in a couple of days ago."

"Could you connect me to his room?"

The man sighed. "Hold on," he said. There was silence and then a ringing sound. Once. Twice. Three times. Four.

It went on and on with no answer.

Claire felt her neck stiffening. She hung up, then called the main number again. The same man answered, *"Motel!"*

"Hi, um, it's me again, Miles Holiday's daughter." She waited for the man to scold her, or at the very least, grunt, but only the sound of a bad connection hissed in her ear. "There was no answer. Can you connect me to the room of his assistant, Clementine Beyers?"

"Hold on—" the man started to say.

But Claire shouted an interruption. "Wait!"

The man cleared his throat.

"Can I leave a message with you as well?" Lucas's words rang through Claire's mind . . . *He might be in real trouble.* "Can you tell my father to call me as soon as possible?"

The sound of pen scratching against paper came through the receiver. "That it?"

"Yes, thank you."

"Do you still want me to—"

"Put me through? Yes, please."

Clementine's phone rang for a while, but the woman did not answer either.

Claire placed the receiver down, feeling worse than when she'd picked it up. She glanced at the clock. It was a little after four. The wait for the motel manager to pass along her message might send her down a familiar, terrifying spiral of worry.

Waiting was the worst.

Why had Lucas planted such an awful seed in her head? What a horrible thing to do. He didn't know her at all, didn't have a clue about the countless nightmares in which she lost her father. Claire never told anyone about her deepest fears. Her friends would have only looked at her funny, as if she were some pathetic creature whose crate was marked *Special Handling*. Then not only would she be the ghost hunter's daughter, but she'd also be *damaged*.

There was another number Claire knew she could

call. She dragged open several desk drawers until she found what she was looking for—a card with the number for the television production office—the people who made her father's show, *Invisible Intelligence.*

A woman with a cheerful voice answered.

"Hi, Debbie. It's me, Claire."

"Claire?" Debbie's voice went cold. "What can I do for you?" It felt like snow was coating Claire's shoulders, and it sent shivers across her skin.

"I was wondering if anyone's heard from my dad. I can't seem to get in touch with him."

The receptionist was quiet for a long time. Just when Claire began to worry that the call had dropped, Debbie answered. "Has no one reached out to you yet?"

"Reached out to me about what?" The shivers became pinpricks.

Debbie paused. "Let me put you on with the boss lady."

Seconds later, Miles's producer, a woman named Layne Redon, was spurting words into her ear. "Claire, I'm so sorry, we meant to call you as soon as we heard, but we've been in touch with the authorities and—"

"Authorities?" Claire interrupted. The pinpricks were making her skin feel numb. "What are you talking about?"

Layne sighed. "Clementine Beyers contacted our office this afternoon. Apparently, your father took off on his own yesterday morning. She hasn't seen him since."

"He . . . disappeared?"

"Disappeared? Oh, no, no, no, sweetheart. I'm sure it's nothing like that. We told Clementine to stay calm, but she insisted on going to the police. So now we're in touch with them too. No one in Hush Falls seems to be worried."

"Except for Clementine."

Layne was quiet for a moment. "Miles will return, Claire. This isn't the first time he's gone off chasing clues by himself."

The numbness was spreading down Claire's legs, binding her feet to the ground. "I . . . I hope you're right, Mrs. Redon."

"Of *course* I'm right!" Layne exclaimed. "Listen, is your aunt Lizzie there? I'd like to let her know what's going on too." Claire answered yes. "Great. We'll be in touch with you as soon as Miles makes contact, and we're not leaving the office tonight until we get word from at least *someone* in Hush Falls." She forced a chuckle. "Don't you worry. Okay?"

Later, after Aunt Lizzie hung up with Layne, after she'd visited Claire in her bedroom to reassure her (poorly) that there was nothing to worry about, Claire sat alone at her desk, staring out the window at the silent neighborhood.

The sky grew pale before darkening—the sun already deep below the horizon.

Claire felt like her soul had been split in two. Part of her was flat certain that Layne was right, that her father would be calling in to say good night at any moment. But the other part of her was a jutting mountain unable to bear its own weight, ready for a landslide.

Aunt Lizzie had made a meat loaf for dinner, but Claire couldn't bring herself to go down to the dining room. Her stomach hurt. Tears were welling inside her head. She clamped down on the feeling, refusing to let it choke her.

Outside, stars winked into existence. A black crown, covered in a million silver jewels, slipped down onto the dome of sky. Claire wished she could be up there in a ship, fighting evil aliens with the characters in the book in her backpack.

At least during space wars, you knew when you were supposed to be scared.

Just over the spindly line of trees across the street, a pair of stars seemed to blink at her. Claire perked up. The stars swayed in the sky. They winked away for a second and then came back again. Little bumps rose on the back of Claire's neck as she realized that the lights were not stars. In fact, they weren't even located in the sky.

The glowing pinpoints were a reflection in her bedroom window.

A pair of glistening eyes.

Eyes fraught with tears.

Someone was standing in the bedroom.

Right behind her.

Claire spun in her chair, swiping at her desk, scattering pens and pencils across the floor.

But there was no one else in the room. She was alone.

In the window, the pinpoint lights had disappeared.

"Mom?" Claire whispered. "Is that you?"

She held her breath.

"Mom?" she asked again. "Did you visit Lucas with a message for me? Is Dad really in trouble?"

She waited for an answer.

"Mom?" Claire tried. "Mom? *Are you there?*"

Chapter Six

LATER THAT EVENING, Lucas sat down to write a letter to his parents.

HELLO, PARENTS!

I'VE BEEN THINKING ABOUT YOU A LOT LATELY. I HOPE YOU'RE BOTH SAFE. GRAMMA IS GOOD, AND SO AM I. HOW'S THE WORK COMING ALONG? DO YOU THINK THAT MORE PEOPLE WILL BE ABLE TO MOVE BACK TO THE CITY SOON? ARE THEY REALLY

GOING TO HAVE TO TEAR DOWN
THAT BIG SKYSCRAPER I READ
ABOUT IN THE NEWSPAPER?

I MISS YOU A TON. THERE
ARE SOME THINGS HAPPENING
HERE I WISH WE COULD TALK
ABOUT. WHEN WILL THE PHONE
LINES TO THE CITY BE UP AND
RUNNING AGAIN? ISN'T THAT
ONE OF YOUR PROJECTS, MOM? I'D
TAKE A BUS DOWN TO SEE YOU,
BUT GRAMMA WOULD LITERALLY
MURDER ME. BESIDES, I'D HAVE TO
SNEAK THROUGH GATES AND
BARRIERS, AND I'M PRETTY SURE
ALL THE TOXIC JUNK ALONG THE COAST—

A soft rapping at the front door nearly knocked Lucas
out of his chair at the kitchen table. His pen went off in
a long black jag across the paper. His mind whirled as
he turned to the front door.

Another visitor already?

He tried to make out a silhouette behind the gauzy curtain, but then Irene called to him from the living room, "Are you expecting anyone, Lucas?"

"No," he answered, his body turning from ice back into water.

Maybe the knocker was an actual living, breathing human being . . .

Irene got up from the couch where she'd been reading a mystery novel and peered out the front window. Lucas heard her let out a little gasp. She unlocked the door quickly and opened it a crack. "Claire Holiday? Is that you?"

Lucas stood up. He felt suddenly lost—the familiar surroundings of his grandmother's kitchen were unrecognizable.

"Yes, ma'am. I'm sorry to bother you so late, but I really need to talk to Lucas. Is he home?"

Irene peeked back at him and then swung the front door open wider. "It is late," she said, a sharpness in her voice.

Embarrassment flooded Lucas's cheeks with red. "I'm here!" he called out over Irene's shoulder.

"Come in, come in," said Irene brusquely, waving the girl into the foyer. "Before you catch cold." Lucas raced to meet her. When he saw Claire's pallid face, there was a tingling inside his bones. *Desperation.* But, he wondered, did this feeling belong to Claire or to himself? Irene squinted, glancing between them. "What are you two up to?"

Lucas hadn't told his grandmother about Mrs. Holiday's visitation. Irene had been curt the morning after Otto had knocked. Lucas had wanted to see if he could figure out this *knocking stuff* on his own. "Homework!" he blurted. Irene and Claire both stared at him as if he'd gone nuts. "We have a project tomorrow, and—"

Irene clicked her tongue. "Why are you lying? Don't you know who you're talking to?" She turned back to Claire and raised an eyebrow. "How'd you get here? I didn't hear your aunt pull into the driveway."

"My bike," Claire answered in a whisper. "My aunt doesn't know I left the house."

Irene sighed, but when Claire's lip started to quiver, she softened. "Oh, it can't be as bad as all that." She led her to the couch in the living room. "I'll make some cocoa," she went on soothingly while looking quizzically at Lucas. "You can chat with Lucas about what you need to chat about. I'll leave you alone."

"I'm sorry, Lucas," Claire said after a moment. "I know it's late. I could've called, but . . . I was worried you would've told me we'd talk tomorrow. I couldn't wait that long. You were right. My dad *is* missing." Lucas nodded, trying to seem sympathetic and not I-told-you-so-ish. She told him about her call to the motel. And to the TV production office. "But the scariest part was when I was alone in my bedroom about an hour ago." Claire shuddered. "I felt my mom watching me—her eyes were on my back. Was there anything else she told you? Anything that might point me in the right direction?"

Lucas shook his head.

Claire slumped down into the couch. "What can I do except wait for all the grown-ups to figure it out? You said that my dad's in trouble *now*. If he's missing, I don't want to wait. I *can't* wait."

Lucas's throat went dry. "Sorry. I'm . . . I'm new at this."

"But your grandmother isn't," Claire answered. Dishes rattled in the kitchen. The microwave let out a loud beep.

Lucas flushed. "I didn't tell Gramma what I saw," he whispered.

Claire pressed her lips together. "Is my mother here now? Can you ask her what I need to do?"

He shook his head. "They come with a knock at the door. I have no clue how to flat-out *summon* them."

"Summon whom?" Lucas's grandmother came through the doorway juggling three steaming mugs of cocoa. Lucas and Claire were quiet as she set the mugs on the coffee table. After a moment, Irene plopped down on the couch between them. "No one wants to answer? That's fine." She was using her this-is-not-fine voice. "Claire, would you pass me the phone on the table beside you? I think it's best I let your aunt know where you are."

"Gramma!" Lucas murmured through his teeth at the same time Claire blurted out, "Lucas saw my mother."

Lucas's lungs clenched.

But Irene only squinted at the cocoa mugs and nodded. "I figured it was something like that." She turned to him. "Why didn't you tell me?"

"I didn't want to make a big deal," he heard himself say.

"But it *is* a big deal," said Claire, sitting up. "My mom came to him. She told Lucas that my dad is missing. I checked with the producers of *Invisible Intelligence*. They said that Lucas was right. My dad disappeared in a town called Hush Falls Holler while scouting for an upcoming episode. My friends and I have tried contacting spirits ourselves but we . . . haven't really had any luck." At this, Irene raised an eyebrow, and Claire hurried to add, "Lucas says he doesn't know what to do. Mrs. Kent, can *you* help me?"

Chapter Seven

IRENE STARED AT the steaming mugs of cocoa.

Lucas watched Claire watch his grandmother. Her glasses were large and round, and behind the thick lenses, her eyes looked watery. Her hands were clenched in her lap, her fingers fidgeting.

"Gramma?" Lucas tried, but she waved him off. She was concentrating, looking inward. He'd seen her do this a handful of times, usually after she'd delivered a spirit message to the intended recipient.

Suddenly, Irene stood and hurried to the kitchen. Claire turned and leaned over the back of the couch, peering after her. Lucas whispered, "That means yes."

"She'll help?"

Lucas nodded. Claire settled down and then bit at her lip. There was a clamor from through the doorway— a great banging of metal pots, pans, and tins—as Irene dug inside messy cupboards. "Lucas!" she called out. "Go into my room and fetch a bottle of india ink from the desk."

By the time Lucas returned to the living room, his grandmother had placed a large silver platter in the center of the coffee table. The cocoa mugs were off to the side, now growing cool. Irene stood over the platter, holding a frosty glass container filled with milk. She poured out a small amount onto the platter, just enough to coat the bottom with white. She held out her hand to Lucas, and he passed her the small bottle wordlessly.

Kneeling beside the table, Irene unscrewed the cap and removed the slick black dropper from inside the bottle. Squeezing its end, Irene dropped three spots onto the milk—making a triangle—before closing the bottle and placing it beside the platter. "Come closer," she whispered to them.

Lucas squatted across the table from where Claire settled. Together, the three of them formed another sort of triangle. Irene unfurled the fingers of her other hand, revealing a strange-looking instrument attached to a long silver chain. Its tiny loops were so compact, the chain looked almost like mercury. An oblong-shaped crystal was attached at one end. It glinted darkly in the dim living room.

"What is that?" Claire asked.

"A pendulum," Lucas answered. "It's supposed to—" Irene flicked a glance between them. Claire flinched. Lucas blushed. His grandmother needed silence.

She grabbed the end of the chain and lifted it away from her palm. Once the chain was taut, the crystal dangled slightly from the pendulum's base. She placed its point inside the trio of ink blots, then moved her hand in a figure-eight motion. The crystal swirled the ink, combining the lights and darks, turning the silver platter into a shifting piece of abstract art. Irene stared down at the swirls as if watching for a sign.

Then the focus of her eyes shifted. She was seeing something in the ink patterns that Lucas could not. And as the pendulum swung, a sense of fear infiltrated her gaze. Irene's eyes grew wide. Then wider. Her lips parted, and she let out a small breath. "No," she whispered. "Oh no." Her head dipped closer to the platter. Then the pendulum leapt away from the ink and milk. The chain slipped from her fingers and clattered to the coffee table.

Irene gasped. Lucas and Claire flinched backward. When he glanced at the platter again, the ink had spread away from where it had been swirling and clung darkly to the platter's silver edges, leaving the remnants of milk gleaming upward as if it were an opaque mirror. Irene rested her fingertips on the lip of the table and released a long sigh. Whatever window she had opened was now closed.

Lucas dared to speak. "What did you see?"

"I saw . . . something that should not be."

Claire's skin had a greenish hue. She pressed her lips together. "Is my father okay? Is he safe?"

"That, I could not say. But the town he was scouting, Hush Falls. It is a bad place."

"What did you see that *should not be*?" Lucas asked.

"I sensed . . . spirits. Many spirits. But there was only one . . . identity."

"I don't understand," said Claire.

"One identity?" Lucas echoed.

"There are many dead people in Hush Falls. But, there is a single spirit, an evil man, whose presence is powerful. His soul is like a magnet. Keeping all the other spirits there." Irene pressed her fingers against the coffee table. "I tried to connect with them. To get a closer look, but the man . . . he *pulled* at me. It hurt."

"Gramma, are you okay?" Lucas asked.

Irene nodded. "Just a bit of a headache now. But if I had stared for much longer . . ." She grimaced and pushed the silver platter away.

"What does that have to do with my dad?" Claire insisted.

"I doubt it has anything to do with him. Except—" Irene stared at Claire. "Your mother, Penelope . . ."

"Yes?" Claire implored.

"She protects you. She protects your father. But in this case . . . she can't." Irene cleared her throat. "And if she were to try, she could become stuck there like the others. She might lose herself. She might . . . forget."

"So then"—Lucas sat up straight—"Penelope came to *me* because she needs us to go and help Mr. Holiday."

"No!" Irene snapped. "We're not going there."

"But, Gramma—"

"Hush Falls is like no other place I've ever glimpsed. It is not safe for people like *us*, Lucas, to go anywhere near it."

"What about for people like me?" Claire asked. "Did my mother visit Lucas because she thinks that there's something that *I* could do? Am I the one who's supposed to find my father?"

Irene sat very still. Lucas could tell she was holding back some secret thought, but he'd never call her out in front of Claire. It must be secret for a reason. "Honey, I think it would be best for the authorities to handle whatever needs to be handled here. There are plenty of capable adults who are experts at—"

"But my mother didn't visit anyone else. She came to see Lucas."

"And the man, Gramma," Lucas interjected. "The bad man from your vision, who you said is keeping all the spirits in Hush Falls prisoner. *Capable adults* won't be able to do anything about him. What if he's the one who—"

"I said no." Irene stood. She snatched the pendulum from where it had landed on the coffee table. Then she lifted the platter so roughly, some of the liquid sloshed out onto the floor. "Shoot. Now I've got to clean that before it stains."

"You're a capable adult, Gramma!"

Irene said nothing but turned and brought the platter into the kitchen. Lucas could not just let it go. "You're the one who told me about my *gift*. What's the point of having it if I can't do anything with it?" Claire was looking at him funny, as if he were suddenly speaking a language she did not understand.

Irene returned with a roll of paper towels and a spray bottle filled with an amber liquid. She crouched, sprayed, and then scrubbed at the spot where the milk and ink had spilled.

"Gramma! Answer me!"

Irene slammed the bottle onto the floor. With a blank expression, she stood and went to the phone. Flipping through a small notebook, she held her finger in place, then dialed the number she'd located. After a moment, she spoke. "Yes, hello, Lizzie?"

"Oh no," Claire whispered.

Lucas's grandmother went on. "Irene Kent calling. I don't mean to alarm you, but I thought you should know that your niece rode her bike up to my house . . . No, no problem at all, but it's time for her to head home, and I don't want her on the dark roads this late . . . Yes, of course. We'll all be waiting." Irene laid the receiver back on the cradle. "I'm sorry, Claire. But I don't allow Lucas to have friends over while he's disrespecting me. Your aunt Lizzie said she'd be here in a few minutes."

Claire stood. "But what about what you saw,

Mrs. Kent? Can't you at least call the police for me? Maybe point them in the right direction?"

Irene softened again. "I will call. Tomorrow. But . . . honey, I'm not sure how much help I'll be."

Claire went over to her. She wrapped her arms around the small woman. Irene stiffened at first, but then she hugged the girl back. "It's going to be okay. Your father's a smart man. I'm sure he knows exactly what he's doing."

Lucas caught his grandmother's gaze. The worry he saw in her eyes told him that she was anything but sure. In fact, he knew she was lying.

Chapter Eight

LATER, LUCAS FOUND himself holding his breath. He was underwater, deep down, pressure pushing at his eardrums. Darkness surrounded him, thick and fathomless. Even though he was certain this was a dream, the water stung his eyes. He kept them open, sensing his body turning in the gloom while looking for an object he could focus on to quell his dizziness. His lungs ached, and when he gasped, he felt his chest fill with a thick type of oxygen.

Not far below, Lucas made out a building. A church maybe. The structure had a steeple. Or a tower.

Lucas's mind rushed to his parents working in the

drowned cities, and fear gurgled in the back of his throat. Was this a vision of the future? Another terrible perk of the *gift* he'd inherited from Gramma? Should he be worried that more waves might come and catch the workers and volunteers on the coast with no warning?

He glanced upward, looking for the surface of the water, wondering if he were to break through into open air, would he wake himself up? But before Lucas could kick away from the building that lurked beneath him, there came a knocking sound. It resounded through the darkness like sonar, pulsing through his flesh and vibrating his bones. Pinpricks poked into his skin. He felt himself being dragged down, down, down. The pressure in his ears grew worse as the knocking became louder.

He wanted to call out, but who would hear him?

A soft sensation coated his feet. He was standing in muck at the bottom of the lake. The building rose up over him now, and he could see it clearly. Not a church, but a house. A mansion, like something from an old black-and-white horror movie. The double doors at the front porch were closed tightly.

Lucas realized then that the sound—the knocking—was not coming from inside the structure. It echoed from somewhere behind him. He allowed himself to turn. To take in the landscape.

The pinpricks dug deeper into his skin, and he almost shrieked at the pain. Spread out before him, lit dimly as if by some mysterious and distant light, was a graveyard. Headstones jutted up from the ground, many of them tilting this way and that. He tried to jump away, to kick and swim, but some strange gravity was holding him down.

He knew somehow that the knocking would end only when he'd located its source. And only then, he figured, would this nightmare be over. Stepping through the mud, Lucas felt weeds brushing at his legs. Something darted past his face. A fish? Or could it have been something else? Something he did not wish to imagine?

Soon, he was standing among gravestones. It was too dark to make out any of the names engraved on them. But the names weren't important. It was the sound that drew Lucas onward. He walked, slowly pushing against the water's weight, until he came to a hole in the ground.

An open grave, its edges crumbling and drooped like a rotting wound. Looking down, Lucas could see an ancient wooden casket at the bottom.

Tap . . . Tap . . . Tap . . .

The noise was coming from below, from inside the box. Lucas drew his hand to his mouth to stop a scream.

Then the casket's lid rose upward and released a cascade of bubbles.

As well as a low groan.

Lucas sat up in bed, flailing with the blankets, gasping for breath.

Sweat was beaded on his forehead. He wiped it away with shaky fingers.

Blinking, he watched his bedroom form around him. When Lucas swallowed, his throat felt like a desert. He needed a glass of water. But as he swung out his legs to stand, he noticed that his bedroom door was already open. The echo of the knocking from his dream sounded slightly in his memory. *Tap . . . Tap . . . Tap . . .*

Had his grandmother come to look in on him? Had she forgotten to close the door?

There was a shuffling sound out in the hallway. He thought of the wavering weeds in the graveyard in his dream.

"Hello?" Lucas whispered.

There was no answer.

Steeling his nerves, he carefully got out of bed. "Mrs. Holiday? Is that you?" Moving quietly across the floor, he hoped that it *was* Claire's mother out in the hall. He didn't think he could handle a different visitor with a new message for a stranger. Creeping toward the doorway, Lucas felt the room tilt, and like in the dream, he had to remind himself to breathe.

A figure stepped from the darkness. A woman. Her hair flowed behind her. Her arms were raised toward him, fingers splayed and trembling hopelessly. Lucas froze. Then, rushing forward like a flood, her terror resounded in his mind. She swung around to clutch his shoulders. Lucas ducked away, crouching and covering his head with his hands.

"Go now!" shrieked the woman. Claire's mother. *"Go! Help him! Please! Before it is too late!"*

*   *   *

Claire couldn't remember falling asleep, but it must have happened, because when sunlight crept across her pillow, she jolted upright. She checked the clock on the table beside her bed. There were at least fifteen minutes left until her alarm would go off. If she were to lie down again, it would only feel more painful later to drag herself from under the covers. So Claire got up, went to the bathroom, and turned the shower knob.

The night before, when her aunt Lizzie had come to pick Claire up at Lucas's house, she'd watched silently as Claire loaded her bike into the car's hatchback. And on the ride home, all that her aunt had said was, "Well, that was embarrassing."

Claire had been too shaken by what had happened in the Kent house to answer, worried that any word would set loose a torrent of tears and trembling cries. Once home, however, Claire had calmed down enough to ask her aunt, "Don't you want to know *why* I went over there?"

"If you feel like telling me, I'll listen." Aunt Lizzie

·**70**·

opened the refrigerator and dug around aimlessly, as if looking for a snack that wasn't there. "But I truly hope this is the last time you sneak out without telling me. I nearly *died* when Irene called."

Claire flinched at the word *died*. "Lucas Kent spoke with my mom." Aunt Lizzie turned to face her, but her expression revealed nothing. Claire scrambled to continue. "Lucas is the one who told me that Dad's in trouble. And I knew that if I'd asked you to take me to Lucas's house, you would have said no."

"Why do you always assume I'm going to say no, Claire?"

"Would you have taken me?"

Aunt Lizzie sniffed. "Well . . . no." Claire struggled to not roll her eyes. "Your father has had enough trouble with that family."

"Lucas wants to help me."

"You don't know Irene Kent like I do. Like *your father* does. The woman is—"

Claire had heard it all before. She spoke up. "Can't we try and find Dad ourselves?"

Mouth agape, Aunt Lizzie looked like Claire had stepped forward and stomped on her foot. "Are you kidding me? You want me to drive us to some creepy backwater so you can tromp around in the woods and—"

"Dad needs me. Mom said so."

"Oh, sweetheart . . ." Aunt Lizzie took Claire's hand. "Let's not jump to conclusions. Your father knows what he's doing. Okay?" Then, as Claire expected, her aunt went on about how the hour was late and that tomorrow would be another long day and wouldn't they both feel better after some chamomile tea and some shut-eye?

Claire had agreed, but only because she didn't wish to argue.

Besides, Aunt Lizzie was right. Tomorrow *would* be another long day. And Claire was not looking forward to it.

If she couldn't get her aunt on board with the idea of going to Hush Falls Holler to look for her father, Claire might have to do something drastic. Something that terrified her more than the thought that Irene Kent could see into the world of the dead—more even than the idea that her father was capable of hunting down the spirit of her mother and sending her away forever.

After her shower, Claire met her aunt in the kitchen.

"Are we feeling better?" Aunt Lizzie asked, handing her a piece of buttered toast globbed with strawberry jam.

"We are," Claire answered with a half smile. She took a quick bite. "I'm sure you're right. We'll hear from Dad before long."

"And then we'll give him a good talking-to!" Aunt Lizzie agreed, offering up her palm for a high five. Claire hated when her aunt did this, but she swallowed a grimace as she swung her hand to smack it. "Do you want a ride to school today or are you okay walking?"

"I can walk."

Aunt Lizzie opened the fridge and pulled out a few plastic containers filled with her lunch. She shoved them into a tote bag, then slung the bag over her shoulder. "Good. I've got an early meeting. You'll be all right alone for a bit?"

"I'm not a baby, Aunt Lizzie."

Her aunt's voice melted slightly. "But you'll always be our baby, Clary." Claire stiffened. Aunt Lizzie was too busy rushing around to notice. "Okay, then. I'll be sure to call the school if Layne reaches out to my office. Till then, fingers crossed!" Claire wanted to scream out that one does not cross fingers in situations like this, but she also wanted her aunt to just leave her alone. "Kisses!" Aunt Lizzie said, and then headed into the garage.

Moments later, silence settled onto the Holiday house, and dread slithered through Claire's veins. She was imagining what drastic thing she might do to help her father, when the doorbell rang.

Peeking out the front window, Claire saw Lucas on the porch, an overstuffed purple backpack strapped to his shoulders. Frazzled, she yanked open the door. "What are you doing here?"

Lucas jumped back in surprise. "I had to come see you before school started. Away from everyone else." He peered past her into the oak-paneled foyer. "Is your aunt home?"

Claire shook her head. "Aunt Lizzie left for work a minute ago."

"Good," he muttered.

"What's wrong?" she asked. "Did you learn anything else?"

Lucas nodded. "She showed up again last night." He glanced over his shoulder, looking past the front lawn to the street. Turning back, he whispered, "Do you see her?"

"Who? My *mom*?" Claire struggled to see what he was seeing. All that was there was the asphalt and the sidewalk and the Mortons' house across the road.

"Your mother followed me here. She . . . she's in my head. She won't leave. I came to ask if you'd mind . . . telling her to leave?"

Yesterday morning, Claire would have turned him away with a scowl. But after the previous afternoon, after what she'd seen at his house with the milk and the ink, after what Lucas's grandmother had said . . . "She's been with you the whole time?" He nodded. "Since last night?" He nodded again. Claire noticed his eyes were glazed over. He must not have slept much. "But what does she want? Did she tell you anything else? Anything about my dad?"

"More of the same. That he's in trouble. And that he needs your help. But this time it was *louder.*"

Claire stifled a nervous giggle. This sounded exactly the way her mother worked. She'd never take no for an answer. Claire tried to imagine her mom standing out in the road. She squinted, trying again to see her. Still, there was nothing. "I asked my aunt to drive me to that town. Hush Falls Holler? She practically laughed in my face."

"And Gramma said it was dangerous." Lucas looked to the street again. "But . . . your mother doesn't care. I can, like, feel what she's feeling. If she doesn't leave me alone, I don't know what'll happen. I worry I might . . . explode or something."

Claire waved him forward. "Come in." She closed the door behind him, then thought for a moment and opened it again. "Is she . . . ?"

Lucas nodded wearily. "She's here." He motioned to

the empty space beside himself. They stood in the hall of the Victorian, surrounded by the antique furniture that Penelope had picked out for her family, the emerald wallpaper, the dark-stained wood, the chandelier made of mercury glass. Even if Lucas *hadn't* told her that her mother had followed him here, it was impossible to ignore the presence of Penelope Holiday. She would *always* be here, just as Miles would always be here, hiding inside the scents of pine and leather and his immense collection of old books.

"Mom?" Claire held her hands out toward the empty space beside Lucas. She wasn't sure what sensation she'd expected to find there. The cool skin of her mother's fingertips brushing against her own? The chime of a spoon hitting against the inside of her mother's favorite tea mug? The feeling of warmth and comfort when her mother would embrace her every morning, the same feeling Claire had realized existed only once those hugs were no longer a part of her life?

What Claire hadn't expected was to feel *nothing* in that empty space. Anger surged through her, and she stepped furiously backward, almost tripping over her own feet. She stared hard at Lucas, knowing that whatever came out of her mouth next would be unfair. *You're lying! She's not here! How come you can see her, but I can't?* Pursing her lips, Claire turned from him. "I don't know what you expect me to do, Lucas," she answered finally. "She isn't haunting me. She's haunting you."

"Just . . . talk to her. Tell her that she's hurting me."

Claire looked back to the empty space, answering flatly, "Mom. Leave Lucas alone. He doesn't want to help us."

Lucas flinched. "That's not true. I do want to help. But . . . I don't know how." He cringed suddenly, as if someone had boxed his ears. He held his hands against the sides of his head. "Stop, Mrs. Holiday. Please stop."

For a brief moment, Claire thought she saw a glimmer in the air. Like ripples of heat rising off asphalt in the summertime. She remembered the previous evening, up in her bedroom, when the stars had blinked at her, when she'd felt her mother's presence. The anger slipped away. And she reached for Lucas, touching his arm. "Mom. Cut it out," she blurted to the empty space. "You're hurting him!"

Lucas's spine snapped straight up. "She says we have to go to Hush Falls."

Claire shook her head, frightened. "I told you. Aunt Lizzie said she wouldn't take me. And your grandmother—"

"It doesn't matter," Lucas answered. His voice had gone strangely low. "She says she won't leave me alone until we find him. You want to go? I know a way."

Chapter Nine

"PACK A BAG," said Lucas. He nodded to his own bulging backpack. "I brought some stuff just in case."

"Just in case what?"

"In case it came to this."

"I thought you came here to tell me to ask my mother to leave you alone."

"I mean, yeah, that was part of it."

"And the other part is?"

Lucas shrugged. "Do you want to save your father or not?" he asked, not unkindly.

Claire glanced up the stairs to her bedroom. There was a canvas duffel in her closet. All she'd need was a few shirts and jeans and she'd be ready to go. "Yes," she answered. "Of course I do. But how? We don't have a car. And you certainly don't have a driver's license."

"There are other ways to get around," he answered. "You've got to hurry. We don't have much time."

Claire wasn't sure what he meant by that. But it got her moving. She ran upstairs, gathered her things, folded them into her bag, and was back down to the foyer in less than a minute.

"Money," he stated seriously. "How much do you have?"

"I don't know. I think my aunt keeps some stashed in the kitchen for emergencies."

"This counts as one. Doesn't it?"

"Won't they be worried about us? My aunt and your grandmother?"

"I'd be freaked out if they weren't. But that's not the point." Lucas shivered. "Isn't your dad's life more important than whether or not our families are nervous for a few days?"

Claire dashed to the kitchen. She opened the antique ceramic cookie jar that was shaped like the head of a grinning clown, then reached in and pulled out several large bills. She waved them at Lucas, who watched from the doorway. He nodded approvingly. "Should we at least leave a note?"

"Saying what?"

"That we're safe? That we'll be back soon?"

Lucas sighed. "It seems like the right thing to do." Then he shook his head. "But it might cut our time short. If we leave, like, now, we'll have all day to travel and figure out the next steps. Once your aunt and my gramma get home, it'll be a few more hours before they realize that we're not coming back today. And then maybe it will be hours after that when they actually do something about it. With a note, they'll know that we're gone, and they'll probably come after us immediately. And if we don't have time to explore Hush Falls, we might never find your father."

Claire's chest trembled. It felt like electricity was zapping through her body. "You're right," she said.

"Are you ready to go?"

She looked around the kitchen. She figured they

might get hungry along the way. So she went to the cupboard and shoved a box of granola bars into her bag. Then she grabbed what was left of the packets of chewy fruit snacks and took those as well. "Maybe I should check with his production company again? See if they've heard from him?"

Lucas sniffed, as if amused. "We already know they haven't."

"How do we know that?"

Lucas's eyes were hard as stones. "Because your mother is still with me."

Hiking toward the center of town, they moved inconspicuously through backyards and side streets. Lucas said he didn't want anyone wondering why they weren't heading toward the middle school for the first bell. He had checked the bus schedule earlier that morning. There was one scheduled to leave for the northern cities within the hour. According to the old road atlas that Lucas's grandmother kept stashed on the bottom of the bookcase in the living room, the bus stop in the middle of the state would get them near to Hush Falls Holler. Though the town was supposed to be surrounded by wilderness to protect the nearby reservoir, there was a state route heading north from the thruway that he thought looked walkable.

They bought tickets at the pharmacy on Maple Avenue, as well as a few bottles of water for their journey. Then they stood at the corner and waited for the bus to arrive.

Claire worried that the driver would question them about traveling alone, especially on a school day, but when he pulled up to the curb, he barely blinked as they handed over their tickets. She climbed the steps and stared down the aisle, empty rows of plush gray seats glaring blindly back at her. Dragging her duffel behind her, she found a spot about halfway back. She was too nervous to try to place her bag onto the overhead rack, so she sat next to the window and hugged the pack to her chest. Lucas slid silently into the aisle seat beside her. The driver climbed back onto the bus and swung the door shut without even glancing at them. It made a quick hissing sound that had Claire clenching her entire body.

"Is my mom . . . Is she . . . ?"

Lucas whispered, "Yeah. She's with us. But she won't be, once we get close to the town. Something there will not let her near."

"Is it the same bad thing that made my father disappear?"

"Not sure. We'll have to figure it out ourselves."

"Is she still hurting you?"

Lucas seemed to gauge himself, then thought for a moment. "Huh. No. Not really. I guess that means we're on the right track? She says she'll keep us safe though, for as long as she can."

The driver put the bus into gear, then moved away from the curb. Claire stared out the window at the familiar town of Archer's Mills, watching as it passed by. Soon, the country roads had taken over the view— budding trees and wet ground and overflowing streams and abandoned stone walls that scratched across the old woods like scars—and she could feel her home disappearing behind her.

Heat was radiating off Lucas's body. He had removed his thick coat and shoved it down into the space behind himself. One of its arms jutted up as if trying to wave at her.

"Are you scared?" she asked him.

Lucas cleared his throat. "It doesn't matter. We'd have to do this whether we're scared or not."

All the anger and the confusion she'd felt toward him only yesterday seemed to evaporate from her mind. He didn't have to do this, she thought. He could have told her where to go. Could have sent her off on her own. But here he was beside her. Choosing to come along on this journey. She felt so grateful that she suddenly wished to give him a hug. But she didn't want to scare him. Instead, she turned and whispered, "Thank you for this."

Lucas flinched. He shook his head, ignoring what she'd said, then he changed the subject. "What do you know about Hush Falls?" he asked. "Why was your father there in the first place?"

Claire sighed, disappointed that he hadn't seemed to hear her. She opened her duffel and pulled out the folder she'd put together the previous evening, stuffed with the notes she'd taken in her father's study. There were names and dates and questions and possible answers. She scanned what she'd written, flipping through some of the papers she'd swiped from her father's desk. "As usual, he was investigating some reportedly strange happenings. This town, Hush Falls, is meant to be super-*duper* haunted."

"Haunted by who?" Lucas asked.

"Well, according to my dad's notes, it's a little complicated. The reason he'd gone to visit the town was to gather a little more information before he brought the whole production team with him."

"What kind of information?" he asked.

"Its history, I guess. The town was founded centuries ago by a family called *Hush*. Hence, the name Hush Falls. I'm not sure if there are any waterfalls in the immediate area. Maybe someone was just being cute. Get it? *Hush Falls?*"

"I get it." Lucas forced a smile.

"A long, long time ago, the Hushes were wealthy traders. Fur, animal oils, *bones*. A bunch of them established estates up there. Big houses. Farms. Over the years, most of the wealth stayed in the family. But in the early 1900s, the state decided to dam up the river downstream from where they lived to create a water supply for the cities that were growing closer to the coasts. Which meant—"

"The town would flood," Lucas added, looking at the seat back in front of him, his face aghast.

"Right," Claire went on. "The state offered to help reestablish the whole town up in the nearby hills. The Holler, they called it."

"Hush Falls Holler," Lucas whispered to himself.

"There wasn't much that the town, or the Hush family, could do to fight. My dad's notes said: *When the state wants your land, they take it.* Almost all the townspeople fell in line. Some of the buildings were demolished and then rebuilt on new streets in the nearby hills. Some houses were moved piece by piece. But the story says that there was one man, an elderly relative of the town's founders, who refused to move. His name was Lemuel Hush. He fought the state to keep his mansion, which was one of the original buildings his ancestors had built on that land. His home was so old that there was even a family graveyard in the woods behind it, and he—"

Lucas flinched. "Wait, what did you say?"

Claire was unsure of which part he'd seemed to have missed. "There was a graveyard? Behind the mansion?"

Lucas's skin had turned grayish. "I . . . I had a dream last night," he stammered. "About a mansion. And a graveyard. They were both underwater. I heard a *knocking* sound coming from inside a coffin. When it opened *by itself*, I woke up. That's when I saw your mother again. In my house. In the hallway outside my bedroom."

Claire cringed. She hated thinking about her mother as a *thing* that could scare someone. "Do you think the dream has something to do with my father?"

"I'm not sure," Lucas answered. "Tell me the rest of the story."

"There's not much left. Mostly just spooky tales passed down through the years. I think my father was trying to figure out if they were true or not."

"What happened to the old man?" Lucas asked. Lowering his voice, he added, "Mr. Hush."

"He got sick. He died. His family blamed the legal battle with the state. It was too much for him to take on at his age. His family buried him in the graveyard behind his mansion as he'd wished. Then the state built the dam just a few months later. Lemuel Hush's house and lands were drowned in the new reservoir. People say the mansion is still down there. Deep and dark and impossible to reach."

Lucas's skin seemed to become even more gray. His voice wobbled. "And the scary tales?"

"They claim that Mr. Hush's ghost haunts the lake. The *reservoir*. They say he's angry about what the state did to him. To his family property." This next part was especially difficult to get out. "Supposedly, lots of people have drowned there."

Lucas sputtered, "Do you think—" but then he

stopped. His face flushed, and his jaw opened and shut several times.

Claire knew what he'd almost said. It felt better to finish the thought than to leave it hanging. "Do I think that's what happened to my father?"

Lucas closed his eyes, then nodded.

"I don't know." Claire allowed her gaze to shift around the empty bus. "What does . . . what does my *mom* think?"

Lucas shoved the arm of his jacket down under the armrest. "That's the weird thing. She won't tell me."

The bus shifted gear and jolted forward, throwing the two of them back against their seats as it pulled onto the thruway and sped up with the traffic.

~ PART TWO ~

THE HOLLER

Chapter Ten

THEY WALKED IN silence along the quiet state route, heading north from the thruway.

Claire and Lucas had gotten off the bus when it had stopped to pick up more passengers an hour and a half from where they'd begun. Lucas had asked at a general store near the stop which direction would lead them to Hush Falls Holler. The young woman behind the counter had raised an eyebrow when she'd pointed up the road, which made Lucas want to get away from there as quickly as possible. Though they'd been walking for a long time, it was still morning. Lucas had no idea how much longer it would be till they reached the town.

It wasn't that they had nothing to say to each other. They'd certainly filled their time on the bus with conversation—about Lucas's parents' recovery work, about Claire's mother's illness. But now, surrounded by tall pines that bowed in the breeze, a chill had come over both of them, and the seriousness of what they had done, what they were doing, sealed their lips shut.

Tree branches creaked. Birds sang deep in the woods. The wind itself was like a mournful chorus, moving over the hills that were growing steeper by the step. Their shoes scuffed along the gravelly shoulder of the road, adding soft percussion to the concerto that Mother Nature was creating especially for them. The sun gazed down from overhead, keeping their shadows close to their bodies.

All the while, Lucas had felt Penelope nearby. Now, however, there was a shift, as if a magnet lodged in his chest was starting to pull him backward, toward the direction from which they'd come. Lucas stopped and Claire stopped too, looking at him with worry. "What is it?" she asked.

Lucas glanced back. Down the road, he could see a blur of movement. When he squinted, the blur took form—a smudge of shadow in the shape of a person. "Your mother," he whispered. "She won't come any farther."

Claire looked back too. "Mom?" she called out. "What's wrong?"

"I think we're getting too close," Lucas answered. "She can't keep up with us. There's something ahead that's stopping her."

Claire shivered. "Should we turn back?"

Lucas closed his eyes and listened. It wasn't a voice that he was hearing—more like thoughts vibrating through his spine, tingling their way out to his fingers and toes. But they weren't his thoughts, he knew. They were *hers*. "No," he said. "She expected this would happen. It's why she needed us to come here in the first place." He waited until the tingling faded. "She wants us to go on. Alone."

Claire clasped her rib cage. "I don't want to be alone."

"We have each other. We can do this." Claire's mom

was gone now—both the blur of her down the road and the non-voice that had been speaking to him through his nerves. It felt suddenly strange thinking she wasn't with him anymore. She'd been the one driving them forward. Though he'd found her presence frightening at first, she'd almost been a comfort since getting on the bus, and Lucas was certain things would only get scarier without her along for the rest of the journey. "Come on. Let's keep going."

Farther along, the sound of an approaching truck growled out from behind them. They darted off the road, into the shadows between the trees, and then waited for the vehicle to pass. Can't be too cautious, Lucas thought. People might already be looking for us. A red pickup zoomed by, the driver not seeming to notice their hiding spot.

When the burping of the engine had faded away, another sound took its place. This one came from the forest, *rat-a-tat*, like a woodpecker. The wind picked up, and Lucas felt a sense of unease. He turned toward the woods.

Someone was standing just down the slope. A man dressed in gray pants, black boots, and a thick overcoat with a burst of black fur at the collar. Dark hair was slicked into a severe part at the side of his head. His eyes were dark, hidden in pockets of shadow, and his mouth was a deep straight gash carved just below his long nose. Before Lucas could grasp what he was seeing, the man stepped behind a tree and was gone.

"What is it?" asked Claire.

"I—I . . ." But Lucas wasn't sure he should tell her. She'd already said she was scared, and why wouldn't she be? His own heart felt like a sputtering lawn mower inside his chest. He knew who this man was, but he didn't know if he could bring himself to say the name.

Hush. Lemuel Hush.

Had his presence warned away Claire's mother? Was this why she had turned back?

"Lucas, tell me. Please."

He looked into Claire's eyes, the thick lenses of her glasses making them appear massive. It wasn't safe here, away from the road. But Lucas had a feeling it would be even less safe as they headed toward the town. "I thought I saw a man."

"In the woods?"

He nodded.

Claire lit up. "Maybe he knows something about my dad—"

The man had stepped out from behind the tree again, and Lucas squeezed Claire's arm. Now the man was grinning. His face made Lucas feel ice crystallizing his bones. He raised his hand and crooked his finger as if instructing Lucas to come toward him. Strangely, Lucas could feel his feet wanting to obey, to step farther into the brush. But a distant noise stopped him. A whooshing sound. The ground began to tremble. Great cracking booms rang out. The man's smile only grew.

And then Lucas saw it.

The wall of water that was coming upon them, towering at an unfathomable height. Brown and churning, taking up the entire forest in its wake, pushing it forward like a weapon. A tsunami, like the one that had destroyed the coast. The water overtook the grinning man, enveloping him in chaos, and then continued toward Lucas and Claire.

There was nowhere to run. No way to escape. Lucas grabbed Claire's hands and then dragged her to the ground. He threw his arms around her as if he could protect her. He knew it didn't matter anymore. In less than a second, they both would be . . .

They would be . . .

Claire was shivering. Lucas opened his eyes. The forest stood as it had been. There was no water. No flood. No tsunami.

No man.

"Let's get out of here," Lucas said, his voice ragged. He led Claire out to the road, not wanting to look back to the woods again. "We need to keep moving."

Claire stomped her foot. "I'm not going anywhere until you tell me what just happened." She clutched her fingers nervously. "What did you see?"

Lucas told her.

＊　　＊　　＊

They continued up the road. They sipped from their water bottles until the bottles were empty. They devoured the snacks that Claire had packed, hoping for energy. Already, Lucas felt a dull ache in his shins. He noticed that Claire had started to limp.

He was grateful that she'd accepted the story of his vision. She hadn't looked at him like he was lying to her, but she did ask him if he knew what the vision had meant. Lucas didn't have the heart to tell her he thought it was nothing good.

For the first time that day, he worried about reaching their destination. If Penelope was too frightened to follow them this far, then how would they be able to make it? Had this journey been a mistake? What if Lucas saw the grinning man again? What if he brought another vision with him, or worse, something that could *really* hurt them?

At the next hill, Lucas felt out of breath, but he didn't want to pause. Something deep inside him understood what was at stake here—a man's life. Claire's future. He remembered what his grandmother had said about his "gift," that it was his responsibility to help others. Why, he wondered, couldn't he have met a spirit who needed him to return a piece of missing jewelry? If he was meant to make a dangerous journey, shouldn't it have been toward the coast, to see his own mother and father? It didn't seem fair.

But then he remembered: the nightmare, the knocking, the feeling of horror that Penelope had sent coursing through his body when she'd shown up, and how she'd stayed, perched in his mind like Poe's raven from that poem they'd studied in English class.

Lucas tripped, falling forward, catching himself on his hands. He checked his body. Thankfully, he wasn't bleeding. "Are you okay?" asked Claire, helping him to his feet. He picked a few stones out from where they'd stuck to his skin.

"I don't know," he answered, holding back something raging just behind his eyes. What would come if he let go? Tears? Anger? Laughter? He looked at Claire and saw the same things in her face.

"Thank you, Lucas," she said.

"For what?"

"For coming with me. Showing me where to go. And what to do." She stared up the seemingly endless road. "Do you want to take a break?"

"We don't have time," he whispered.

Eventually, buildings began to spring up along the road. Mobile homes with overgrown grass. Cars propped on cinder blocks in long driveways. Cottages that looked like no one had lived in them for decades. When the buildings began to appear at shorter and shorter intervals, Lucas started to hope that they were coming closer to their target—the haunted town of Hush Falls Holler. The trees here seemed to be packed closer together, the brush between them like a barrier keeping anyone from wandering off into the mysteries that lingered in the woods beyond.

Ahead, there was an intersection. On one corner stood a decrepit-looking gas station. The two pumps that huddled in the lot out front looked ancient. Lucas and Claire crossed the road to keep away from the place.

Through a large window, Lucas peered at an older man wearing a beat-up trucker hat sitting behind the counter. He was gazing at a small television screen, which cast flickering light onto his wizened face. Thankfully, the man didn't seem to notice them.

"Which way?" Claire asked.

"Not sure," said Lucas. He tried to recall the map he'd looked at earlier that morning. But then, a few hundred yards past the intersection, he noticed a marker that read *Hush Falls Holler* with an arrow pointing forward. And just beyond that, rising up halfway to the treetops, was an old ornate neon sign, red, white, and blue, but unlit. *Lost Village Motor Lodge.*

Chapter Eleven

"IS THAT IT?" Claire asked. "My dad's motel? We're actually here?" She almost started running toward the parking lot that spread out in front of the wide wood-shingled building, but her body wouldn't allow her to move any faster. Her heels had blisters that were rubbing against the insides of her sneakers. Pain shot both up her calves and down to her toes, so she limped forward, Lucas a few yards behind her.

"Wait, Claire," he called out. "We don't want anyone to see us, remember?"

"Which room was he staying in?" she asked, half to

herself, half to Lucas, as if he would have any clue. "We'll have to ask at the office."

"We can't," Lucas insisted. "They'll wonder who we are, where we came from. They might even call the police."

Claire stopped once she'd reached the lot. She stared at the motor lodge. There were maybe ten rooms in total, each black door opening onto the parking spaces that were marked with yellow on the pavement out front. Jutting from the center of the building was the office. It was surrounded on three sides by big windows so that whoever sat inside could see in three directions. A *Vacancy* sign in the window was lit up in red neon. It made her think of her father, whose room must certainly be vacant now. The motel was tucked into an envelope of dense pines that rose high overhead, casting shadows over the property. A single car was parked at the left side of the lot, directly in front of a room with a large silver *#1* attached to its door. A sporty black roadster. Claire recognized it immediately.

"That's my dad's car!" she exclaimed, then took off across the parking lot, ignoring the pain that was attacking her feet.

Lucas followed closely behind her. He nudged her toward the edge of the lot, closer to the trees. He wanted her to be discreet, but she didn't care. What if her father was in the room near where his car was parked? What if he'd already reappeared? She would burst through the door and throw her arms around him and he'd calm her down and explain exactly what had happened, where he had gone, what he had seen.

"Dad!" she cried out.

"Claire, shhh!" Lucas grabbed her elbow, forcing her to a halt.

Claire pulled away, suddenly enraged. "What if he's in there? What if you were wrong?"

Lucas went stone still. "I'm not wrong."

"Let's see about that." But she trudged forward more carefully now.

When they reached the car, Claire noticed dead pine needles covering the hood and the windshield. In the back of her brain, she knew this wasn't a good sign. It meant the car had been sitting here for some time. She squinted at the trees in anger, as if it were their fault she'd gotten her hopes up.

Lucas was already at the door. She gaped at him as he turned the knob. To her surprise, the door swung inward, revealing a darkness inside that chilled the marrow in her bones. "Lucas, wait!" But he didn't pause. She stopped at the doorway, peering toward the office whose reflective windows hid whatever or whoever might be inside. Shoving away the feeling that someone was watching them, she followed Lucas into room *#1* and closed the door quietly behind her.

The room wasn't as dark as it had seemed from outside, especially after Lucas dragged the thick curtains aside. It was as ordinary a motel room as any Claire had seen. Yes, maybe the furniture was a little dated, the bed cover worn in several spots, the carpet shaggier and more orange than what one might see in a modern home, but everything appeared to be in order. And it was clean, as if her father had never even set foot inside this place.

"Where's all his stuff?" she asked. "His equipment? His luggage? His clothes?"

Lucas pulled open the closet door with a grunt, then stepped aside, as if a body might topple out and crush him. When nothing happened, he reached inside, the sound of wooden hangers clattering hollowly. "Not sure. Maybe . . . maybe this wasn't his room?"

"Or maybe someone already emptied it out," said Claire. Would Clementine, her father's assistant, have done that? Maybe Clementine meant to return the camera and sound equipment to the production company. The thought made Claire sick—what was more important here? The television show or her dad?

A shadow crossed in front of the window, heading toward the door. Claire and Lucas froze. Then quickly, they dropped to the floor, hiding on the far side of the bed. To Claire's horror, the door squeaked open slowly. Without thinking, she clutched Lucas's hand. He squeezed hers back.

Footsteps entered, hushed against the thick carpet.

A light switch flicked on and an amber glow filled the shadows. Whoever had entered was coming closer.

Oh no, oh no, oh no, thought Claire. She'd been foolish to let her excitement shove aside her common sense. Of course they'd been seen coming up the drive. And now it was too late to run, or to try to shuffle underneath the bed. They'd make too much noise.

A shadow spilled onto the floor near the end of the bed, and Claire watched as a pair of shoes came into view. Her heart rose into her throat as she glanced up and saw a girl staring down at them.

Chapter Twelve

"WHO ARE YOU?" the girl demanded. She looked to be around their age. "What are you doing here?"

Claire and Lucas sat up on their knees, both backing against the wall beside the bed. Claire was too stunned to answer. Not because the girl had striking hair so blond that it was practically white or because it sprang out from her head in curls so wide, she looked like a beauty pageant contestant. But Claire had been expecting to encounter the gruff man who had answered the phone when she'd called the motel the previous evening. Or maybe even the one who Lucas had seen in the woods alongside the road—the one who had caused his total meltdown.

The girl frowned. "Um, I *said*—"

"We heard what you said," Lucas answered, finally bringing himself to his feet. "We're just . . . a little freaked out is all."

Now the girl crossed her arms. "*You're* freaked out? I'm the one who just found two kids sneaking around my grandparents' motel. Inside a room that's practically a crime scene. Now, are you going to answer me, or am I going to have to call the police?" She glared down at them.

"No, please," said Claire, using the bed to help herself up. "I'm Claire. This is my friend Lucas. We didn't mean to bother you. Well, I guess we *did* mean to, but . . . we've got a good reason. You see, my dad was a guest here for a few days. Yesterday, we learned that he went missing here in Hush Falls Holler. And Lucas . . . he had a bad feeling. So, we came to see if we could find him. My dad. Maybe you've seen him? Miles Holiday?" The words had streamed from her mouth in an embarrassing tangle, and she didn't blame the girl for gaping at her now as if she were a phantom.

"*You're* the ghost hunter's daughter?"

Claire tensed at the maddening nickname, but she nodded anyway. "We didn't mean any harm. And we're sorry for just barging in. But we don't want anyone to know that we're here. My aunt and Lucas's grandmother think we're at school. We took the bus. Then we walked up from the thruway."

"Wow." The girl sighed, but her big blue eyes stayed wide. "You guys came all this way by yourselves?"

"What would you do to save one of *your* parents?" Lucas asked.

The girl shivered. His words had touched a nerve. "I'd probably do something similar," she answered. After a moment, she smiled, then extended her hand to Claire. "I'm Dolly. I live here at the Lost Village with my dad and my grandparents."

Claire reached out and took Dolly's hand. "Have you seen him?" she asked. "My father?"

Dolly shook her head. "Not in a couple of days. That lady he was with took off last night. She left her number. Said she was going back to the production office."

"Clementine?"

"She was really worked up." When Dolly noticed Claire's nervous reaction, she scrambled to add, "But I'm sure your dad's fine! People go missing around here all the time!"

"And then they turn up?" Lucas asked hopefully.

Dolly's face flushed. "Well . . . no." Her eyes bugged out as she realized what her words had meant to Claire. "Mr. Holiday will come back. He looked so . . . clever."

Claire slumped down onto the mattress. Sitting, she put her face in her hands and sighed heavily through her fingers.

"We're here to find Claire's dad," said Lucas, nodding toward Claire. "We could use some help."

"I'm good at helping!" Dolly sat next to Claire and put her hand on her shoulder. Claire flinched, then looked up. Her eyes were red from holding back tears. "What can I do?"

"Do you have Band-Aids?" Claire reached down to untie her sneakers and winced at the pain. "My feet are all messed up."

"Sure. Gram and Gramps have a first-aid kit over in the office."

"Won't they want to know why you need it?" Lucas asked.

"Oh, they're not here right now. The mayor's having a meeting at the town hall about—" She bit her lip and glanced at Claire. "About your dad. He says the town needs a plan."

Claire perked up. "People are going to search for him?"

"Well, no, at least not yet. The mayor says that we need to be ready for when the news gets ahold of this story. That we need to prepare for visitors."

Claire scoffed. "Visitors?" She shook her head. "You mean, like reporters?"

"And curious folk, I guess. I know, it's gross." Dolly added, "I'm so sorry." She stood. "Let's go to my room. I'll take care of you there. Band-Aids. Ointment. The whole shebang. Then we can figure out what to do next. About your dad, I mean."

"Thank you," Claire whispered. She threw her arms around the girl's shoulders and squeezed, grateful for the surprising kindness.

Chapter Thirteen

LUCAS FOLLOWED THE girls along the curb at the front of the motel. They reached the office, and when Dolly went inside to grab the first-aid kit, he couldn't help but peek. On the front desk were books and ledgers and piles of papers. The wood-paneled wall at the rear made the small room look even smaller than it already was, and with the lights off, the poor motel seemed abandoned and somewhat lonesome.

Haunted, maybe.

But then, everywhere felt haunted lately.

He glanced out to the road, fearful that some resident of this village might spot the three of them. He was *more* fearful of seeing the spirit that had come to him out in the woods and brought that terrifying flood into his brain—Lemuel Hush. He knew that Mr. Hush had been trying to make him think of his parents, to exploit his fear of another tsunami striking the coast where they were stationed. And it had worked. Was still working.

Lucas wondered what might have happened during the vision if Penelope had been with them. Would she have helped him fight Hush off? Could ghosts do that sort of thing?

Claire was limping worse than before, and Lucas wished he were strong enough to carry her so they could get back inside and out of sight. But Dolly took her hand and led her into the room at the very end of the motel. The wind rushed through the woods beyond the parking lot, and for a moment, Lucas was certain that someone or something was watching. Then he ducked quickly through the doorway.

"Wow," Claire exclaimed once Dolly had closed the door and turned on the retro-looking lamps that were scattered throughout the space. The same orange shag carpet as in Miles's room covered the floor. On the wood-paneled walls hung half a dozen posters, held by pushpins, of a woman with sparkly makeup and enormous blond hair.

Dolly saw Lucas looking. "My mom loved Dolly Parton. That's where my name comes from. I want to be a singer and a songwriter just like her. I'm pretty good. I've made a few tapes of myself that I thought I could send to the radio stations."

Lucas felt the need to tell her that he didn't think radio stations worked that way, but he didn't want to be rude. Besides, maybe she was right. Lately, anything seemed possible.

"You have this whole room to yourself?" Claire asked.

Dolly nodded proudly. "I was living in a room with my mom and dad until just last year. But then my mom . . . Well, she passed away. That's what Gram says to say. It's nicer than *she died*." She glanced between Claire and Lucas, as if assessing them. Lucas didn't know how to respond. Despite his new ability to see ghosts—to talk with them, even—mentioning death still made him feel strange. "After that, my dad thought it would be better if I took a room of my own. And let me tell you: I did *not* complain."

"What if a whole bunch of guests arrive all at once?" Lucas asked. "What if they need your room?"

Dolly shrugged. "Hasn't happened yet."

"But didn't you say the mayor expects tourists to show up? Once *word gets out* about Miles being missing?" Claire threw Lucas a dirty look, and he felt his face flush. He hadn't meant to make Dolly feel bad about what she'd said earlier.

"I hadn't really thought about that," Dolly answered. "But I guess Gram and Gramps will deal with it if it happens. Just like everything else life has thrown at us."

Claire sat on Dolly's tightly made bed and said, "I'm sorry to hear about your mom. My mother passed away a little while ago too."

"I know," Dolly whispered. "Your dad talks about Penelope all the time on his show."

"Oh," said Claire. "So you're a fan?"

"Sorta. Isn't everybody? Why don't you take off those shoes and socks." She headed over to the sink and wet a washcloth before returning to Claire's side and popping open the first-aid kit.

Lucas flinched when he saw the spots of blood that had soaked through Claire's socks. But Dolly went right to work, rinsing the backs of Claire's feet with the cloth and applying iodine and ointment to the raw skin before covering the wounds with thick wads of protective gauze, which she kept in place with extra-large Band-Aids. Claire impressed him with how calm she stayed, barely wincing at Dolly's gentle prodding.

"You're a good nurse," Lucas said to Dolly.

Dolly smiled at him. "I know a thing or two about a thing or two."

Claire reached into her duffel bag, pulled out a pair of clean socks and slipped them on, then wiggled her toes with ease. "Much better. Thank you," she said. "So tell us about the town. Do you know anything about Lemuel Hush?"

Dolly's smile dropped. "Everyone in Hush Falls Holler knows about him."

"Right. He's your local legend. We have some of those in Archer's Mills too, though my dad doubts that any of them are legit."

"Mr. Hush isn't *just* a legend. He's real. Like, *really* real."

A gust of wind barraged the front of the motel, and the three were silent for a moment.

"Have you ever seen him?" Lucas asked.

"No, thank goodness. They say if you see him, it's already too late. Most times anyway."

Lucas's mouth felt suddenly sandy. "I saw him," he answered. "Earlier today. In the woods just off the highway."

Dolly stood, then skittered quickly away from the bed where they had been sitting. "You *saw* him?"

"I think so. Tall guy. Dressed in a thick wool coat. Collar lined with fur."

"That's him. His picture hangs in the Hush Falls Museum just down the street."

"There's a museum here?" asked Claire.

"I mean, it's not ever open. No one comes through the Holler much anymore. But yeah, it was one of Mr. Winterson's businesses. He opened that one awhile back to try and get people to visit. Tourists visit the towns all around this area. Dad says we're a little too far off the beaten path to benefit. We'd move but . . . there's just not enough money at the moment."

Claire blinked. "Who's Mr. Winterson?"

"The mayor. Everyone round here just calls him Reed. Except for me. He was never very nice to my mom when she was alive." Dolly glanced at Lucas. "Did Mr. Hush say anything to you when you saw him?"

"No. He just smiled. And sort of gestured for me to come closer. And then . . ." Lucas shivered, remembering the wall of water that he'd seen rushing through the woods. "I had a vision."

"What kind of vision?"

"Of a flood."

Dolly shuddered. "He's angry," she whispered. Lucas and Claire were quiet. They waited for her to continue.

"They say he's trapped here. At the bottom of the reservoir."

Lucas thought of his dream from last night. Of the waterlogged mansion. The flooded cemetery. The open grave and the coffin that was lying at the bottom. Had Penelope sent him that information? Or had Mr. Hush himself been calling?

"Trapped?" Claire echoed. "By what?"

Dolly sighed. "Have you ever heard of a graveyard watch? Before she *passed*, my mother was obsessed with the idea."

"My father wrote those words in his notes," said Claire. "But I didn't know what they meant. What's a graveyard watch?"

"In olden times, people believed that the spirit of the last person buried in a graveyard remained behind, to be a kind of . . . protector. A guide for whomever would be the next to pass. The next to be buried. The graveyard watch would help the spirit of this next person adjust to the afterlife, and then they would move on to whatever comes later. That next spirit would take over the job of graveyard watch. Waiting for the next person to pass. To be buried. And so it would continue, on and on."

Claire lit up. "Mr. Hush was the last to be buried in his family's graveyard before the dam was built. *He* was the graveyard watch. But no one else can be buried there since it's underwater. He can't pass on!"

Dolly nodded expressionlessly. "He's trapped. He's frantic. And he'll do anything to get free."

"Anything?" Lucas asked. "Like what?"

"He hunts for his replacement. They say if you get too close to the water, or at least the part of the reservoir where his mansion sits at the bottom, he'll come up and drag you down."

Claire let out a squeak of shock. She didn't have to say a word; Lucas knew that she had just imagined what might have happened to her father.

After a moment, Dolly went on. "Lots of people have drowned there and that's a fact. It's what happened to my mother." She sighed, her breath coming out in ragged pieces. "They found her in the shallows at the water's edge. She'd gotten it into her brain to explore that area. To see if she could find a way to stop Lemuel Hush. Or set him free. She believed that *he* was the reason people were staying away from Hush Falls Holler. That if she could do something about him, tourists would come and the motel would start making money again."

"How did she think she could set him free?" asked Lucas.

"By continuing to use that graveyard. So that Mr. Hush would no longer be the last one buried there. So that he'd no longer be the graveyard watch."

"Do you . . ." Claire stammered. "D-do you think that what happened to your mother is what happened to my father?"

Dolly sat again on the edge of her bed. It seemed to Lucas that the blond woman from the poster on the wall behind her was looking down at her pityingly. "I mean, I can't say I haven't thought about it. But . . . I really don't know."

Chapter Fourteen

LUCAS KNEW THAT if they didn't stay on task, their fear could overtake them and they'd become paralyzed. How easy would it be to simply call his gramma and tell her to come pick them up? "Did you notice who Mr. Holiday was talking to while he was here?" he asked Dolly. "Or maybe some of the places he visited?"

"Or where his equipment went?" Claire added. She must have had the same idea that he did, because her brow was furrowed, and she looked suddenly determined. "His room was empty just now. Did Clementine, his assistant, take his things with her?"

Dolly shook her head. "The police chief scooped up

all the stuff that your dad had in his room and brought it to the station."

"That's weird," said Claire. "Why wouldn't they just leave it for him? In case—" She cleared her throat. "In case he comes back?"

"I'm not sure. I thought it was normal police procedure. Like, for evidence?"

"But if they're not even searching for him yet, why would they worry about evidence?" Lucas asked.

"Is the station nearby?" Claire cut in. "Maybe we can go ask for it back? We could review whatever footage he recorded. I bet there's a clue in there somewhere."

"Going to the police would be like walking into a lion's den," Lucas said, shaking his head. "We don't want anyone to know we're here. Remember?"

Claire frowned. "Of course I remember." She turned to Dolly. "But we have help now. Right, Dolly?"

"Indeed! I know all the officers. Well, there are only two of them, but still . . . *I know them.*"

"I doubt they'd just *hand over* confiscated equipment," Lucas insisted.

"Then we'll have to find a way to retrieve it without them knowing." Lucas and Claire gazed at Dolly as if she'd just spoken in another language. Steal from the police? Was this girl serious? "I watch the crime shows on TV with my grandparents," Dolly added sheepishly. "I know how these things work."

"Do you really think it's possible?" Claire asked, bending over to put on her sneakers. When she stood, she rotated her ankles, testing for pain. "To get his stuff back?"

"Of course!"

Lucas wished he could have a dose of her enthusiasm.

Dolly told them to leave their things in her room, explaining that, since it was her responsibility to keep the space clean, the rest of her family rarely set foot inside. Out in the parking lot, the blue sky peeked through a wide opening in the trees overhead. The sun had moved a bit farther west, and Lucas felt like time was passing faster than ever. It must be close to noon? She led them toward the trees at the edge of the asphalt.

"We're going through the woods?" Lucas asked with hesitation.

"I'm not sure when people will be coming out of the mayor's meeting," Dolly answered, "and I don't want to run into them on the road. There's a shortcut. Don't worry. I know the way." Then she stepped into the brush.

Claire gave Lucas an apologetic look and followed.

The path was dark. Branches from the smaller pines reached out as if to clutch at Lucas's coat. Brown leaves and pine needles carpeted the forest floor. He flinched at practically every noise: the sudden flapping of wings as a startled crow took to the sky, cawing and crying out warnings to its friends; the creaking of barren branches; the sporadic falling of dead twigs from high overhead; the rustling underbrush as small critters dashed out of their way. Lucas glanced around, imagining Lemuel Hush, the graveyard watch, stomping closely behind them.

When they came to a clearing, he stepped onto crumbling asphalt. Looking down, he realized that they were passing through what had once been another large parking lot, the tall grass having broken through the debris. Closer to the road, the remains of a low building stood. Large green letters rose up from the roofline, empty light sockets marking their centers, spelling out *AMUSEMENTS*. Dolly noticed his gaze and explained, "Another one of Mr. Winterson's failed projects. There was an arcade inside. And bumper cars around front. And across the street, he had a mini-golf course filled with the coolest decorations: a pirate ship, a castle turret, and, of course, a bunch of windmills. It's too bad he shut everything down. Now there's *really* nothing to do around here. Except wandering around like *this*." She winked, then waved them forward. "The station is just ahead."

The next lot they entered was the overgrown backyard of a boxy early-American home, dim windows lined up like dominoes. They walked through the rear of the property. More houses stood just ahead. They were nearing the center of the town. Soon they were hiding behind an overgrown hedgerow at an intersection. On the opposite corner was a compact stone church with a small steeple, a general store that looked nearly empty, and another newish building with an entry made of darkened glass. Over the door of this newer building was a sign, *Hush Falls Holler Police*, its dark blue letters standing out against the blond-brick facade.

Dolly stepped out onto the sidewalk, looking both ways. Turning back, she called, "All clear." The three dashed across the street.

Lucas felt totally exposed as he and Claire waited just outside the station's entrance. Dolly was peeking through the glass, her hands up, blocking out the daylight. "The secretary, Mrs. Carmichael, is at the desk," she told them. "She's friends with my gram. I can distract her for a minute. Follow me into the vestibule. When I give the signal, you two head down the hall to the left of the lobby. Hide in the restroom. I'll meet you there and we'll go on to where they keep evidence stuff. Sound good?"

"What's the signal?" Lucas whispered.

But Dolly had already opened the door.

Inside the vestibule, he and Claire pressed themselves

against the wall so that Mrs. Carmichael couldn't see them. The problem was that they couldn't see her either.

"Hi there, Dolly!" came a kindly voice from just around the corner. "What on earth are you doing here? Shouldn't you be home studying?"

"I'm on a break," Dolly chirped back. "Since everyone's still at that meeting, I thought I'd stop in and say hi."

"Well, I'm sure glad you did. It's been a while."

Lucas watched as Dolly headed to the right side of the main desk. "Any update on Mr. Holiday?" she asked. He stared intently at her face, nervous that he'd miss her signal if he looked away.

"Not that I know of. Gosh, it must be hard for you to be part of this."

"Why do you say that?" asked Dolly

"Oh, I'm just thinking of your poor mother. Chief Bray did say they went out to the reservoir to check the shoreline, and thankfully that man, the ghost hunter, was nowhere to be seen. There's still hope."

Dolly turned to them and made her eyes wide, before

facing the desk again with a smile. "Well, that sure sounds like good news to me," she answered cheerily.

Claire nudged Lucas gently in the ribs. "That was the signal." They leaned forward and saw that Mrs. Carmichael's head was turned fully away from them, then they slipped around the corner to find the hallway exactly where Dolly had said it would be.

As they crept across the linoleum floor, Dolly's conversation with the secretary continued. Lucas headed down the passage lit by sickly fluorescent bulbs overhead. A doorway marked *Restroom* appeared on the right. He and Claire snuck inside and switched on the light.

The pale blue walls were made of cinder block. There was a single stained urinal. Beside it, a toilet stall's flimsy-looking door was shut loosely. Lucas caught a glimpse of himself in the mirror and recoiled. His face was red and smudged with dirt. It was the first time he considered how long this day had already been, and he felt himself suddenly overcome with fatigue. Claire stood close to the door, listening for Dolly. He wanted to ask her how she was feeling but didn't want to make any noise that might bring attention to them. Instead, he leaned against the sink, holding his breath, and fought the temptation to run the faucet and clean himself up.

But there *was* the sound of water running somewhere in this small room. A thin skim of liquid shimmered just under the door of the stall. It bloomed outward slowly, creeping tile by tile away from the toilet. Lucas felt his body tense just before the noise echoed softly from within the enclosed space. *Tap-tap-tap.* He'd almost expected it. His grandmother's words rang in his head: *They always come with a knock.*

His vision blurred. His thoughts felt like electric shocks.

Claire's back was to him; she hadn't heard a thing.

The water on the floor continued to spread. Then a ripple passed through the puddle underneath the door, as if someone standing inside the stall had shifted slightly and disturbed it.

Lucas couldn't speak. Couldn't breathe. Couldn't move.

The silver circle on the door began to turn as

someone on the other side unlocked the stall. The door swung outward sluggishly, as if time itself were at odds with Lucas's rapid heartbeat. He watched in horror as the shadowy space inside was revealed, and a dark figure hidden there began to slide forward.

The water spread out quickly now, almost halfway across the bathroom floor.

But the sound . . .

Tap-tap-tap.

The sound of it grew louder—a hollow crashing. Pulsing. Crushing. From far away. But closer. Closer. The wave was barreling toward the station, and Lucas knew there was nothing he could do to escape it.

Chapter Fifteen

CLAIRE WAS HESITANT to press her ear against the grimy door, but she did it anyway. From down the hall, Dolly's voice continued to echo, her words blurry from the distance. Could she maybe hurry this up, Claire thought, then felt immediately guilty. The girl was going out of her way to help, after all.

Another noise caught her attention. An odd groaning. Just behind her.

Ehhh.

Lucas stood rigid next to the sink. His throat was gurgling. His eyes looked glassy, and he stared toward the far side of the restroom where the stall door remained shut.

Claire's first instinct was to reach out and shake him, not because he looked so odd, but because she worried the noise he was making would alert the secretary. As soon as she touched his arm, however, she realized that something was wrong.

He didn't react.

In fact, his gurgling grew louder.

EHHH.

"Lucas!" she whispered harshly. No answer. His eyes were fixated on something she couldn't see. Something by the stall. If he kept this up, Mrs. Carmichael would come running. Claire stepped in front of him, but he stared right through her as if she were invisible. There was terror churning in his eyes. His mouth was an open O. Grabbing his face, she tried to force his jaw shut. But this only made the sound come out of his nose, changed it into a piercing hum. She covered his mouth and nose with her hand. But it didn't help. In a moment, Lucas might start screaming.

Footsteps were coming down the hallway.

Panicked, Claire grabbed his shoulders and turned

him to face the exit. The door began to swing inward. If they didn't move, immediately, whoever this was would spot them. She grabbed him again, holding her breath, then lunged with him toward the wall. After what felt like forever, Dolly's face appeared from around the door. She scrunched up her brow in confusion at the sight of them—Claire's arms wrapped around Lucas's chest from behind—but she didn't say a word before motioning for them to follow her.

Claire turned Lucas around. He blinked at her and then shuddered, coming back to himself. She felt her breath release from her lungs. She hadn't even realized she'd been holding it.

You okay? she mouthed to him.

He nodded groggily.

She wanted to grill him, to ask him what had happened, what he'd seen. But Dolly was watching them impatiently from the doorway, so Claire took his hand and led him out to the hallway, trying not to tremble. When he didn't squeeze her hand back, she grew even more worried. He must have had another vision. A bad one. Had her mother been involved?

Dolly brought them to the end of the hallway and into a cramped room with a murky overhead light. If this was supposed to be an evidence locker, it wasn't very secure. There was a single wall of shelves that reached up to the ceiling, and each shelf was divided into numbered sections. Most of these sections contained boxes or accordion files, but one spot near the bottom was different.

Claire recognized her father's belongings and nearly shrieked with joy. There was his suitcase. And his camera bag! She almost ran over to snatch them up, but then she realized she was still holding Lucas's cold hand. Dolly was staring at them. "What happened to you two?" she asked.

"I don't want to talk about it," Lucas answered, staring at the floor.

"Let's grab my dad's things and go," said Claire, slipping her hand out of Lucas's loose grip. At the shelf, she zipped open both of the bags to see what was inside. "Camera. Tapes. Clothes. I think this is all of it." She stepped back and glanced at the rest of the shelves, making sure she didn't miss anything.

"You saw him again," Dolly said to Lucas. "Mr. Hush."

Lucas turned pale. "He's evil," he choked out, then shifted his gaze quickly to Claire, looking guilty. Claire didn't have the energy to let his words sink in or wonder why he might have said them. She was sick of feeling terrified for her father. Her mother wouldn't have sent her here if there was no hope.

"What's the plan, Dolly?" she asked. "How are we getting out of the station with all this stuff?"

"I told Mrs. Carmichael I needed to use the bathroom. I'll go on ahead and distract her again. When she's not looking, I'll say something like . . . *Good golly, look at the time.* That's how you'll know to sneak back to the vestibule."

Claire handed the suitcase to Lucas. She shouldered the video camera case's strap. Then all three stepped back into the hallway.

Once they'd made it outside to the sidewalk, Dolly rushed them around the corner of the building. "Looks like the mayor's meeting's over," she whispered, nodding to an older couple strolling on the other side of the street. "I don't think they noticed us."

"Should we try to make it back to the motel?" Claire asked.

"Too far. Too many pairs of curious eyes. It's hard to do anything around here without everyone noticing. We should head back just before sunset."

"But that's hours away. And we need to watch my father's footage *now*. How else will we learn where he went?" She looked to Lucas for support, but he was still lost somewhere inside his head, maybe remembering what he'd seen, or maybe seeing something new. New and worse.

Dolly pressed her lips together and let out a soft hum. Then she snapped her fingers and said, "I've got it. Follow me."

She took them along the side of the building, then through a back alley to another overgrown clearing.

Ahead stood a building that reminded Claire of her own house. A Victorian with a turret—only this one looked Gothic and on the verge of collapsing. From the back of it, she took in a screened porch sagging off the rear door, gray paint chipping from wood shingles, and the roofline dipping down in the center like a grim smile.

"What is this place?" Claire asked.

"The Hush Falls Museum." Dolly trod forward, pushing aside the weeds and scrub that tangled up the backyard. "It's closed for the foreseeable future, according to Gram. Sometimes kids in high school will break in here at night. But during the day, we should be fine. The back door is locked but I know a trick to getting it open. It's all in the wrist."

Lucas was struggling with the suitcase, one of his shoulders lower than the other as he grappled with the handle. "The camera bag is lighter," Claire told him. "Do you want to switch?" He shook his head and continued on silently through the brush.

This isn't good, thought Claire. Not good for Lucas. And not good for her father. It had been easy enough for

Dolly to put iodine and gauze and Band-Aids on Claire's blistered feet, but fixing Lucas would be a different story. If there was one thing her father had taught her, it was that ghosts shouldn't be poking around in your head. This was one of the reasons he did what he did—send the spirits packing—so that people could move on with their lives and stop floating in a swamp of the past.

They snuck across the tilting porch. At the back door, Dolly moved the knob in a way that caused the latch to click. She pushed, and the door creaked inward, releasing a stale, dusty aroma that made Claire's sinuses seize. "Here we are," Dolly stated proudly before stepping inside.

Once Claire's eyes adjusted to the dark, she made out that they were in an old-fashioned kitchen.

A woman stood by a wood-fired oven, her back toward them.

Claire nearly fell backward in surprise. Lucas dropped the suitcase, which fell to the floor with a hard whack.

"It's a mannequin," Dolly blurted. "No need to pee your pants."

"What's it doing in here?" asked Claire. The figure wore a long brown dress with a pinafore apron tied at the back. Her hair was done up and hidden underneath a white bonnet. It was difficult to put away the thought that the mannequin might suddenly turn and face them, holding out a plate of cookies like a witch in a fairy tale.

"Reed Winterson set them up, I guess to look like the people who once lived and worked in this house. Like, for education? For when tours come through? *Came* through. Once upon a time."

"The mayor did this?" Claire asked.

Dolly nodded.

Claire walked cautiously around the figure to find a blank face made of white fabric. No eyes. No mouth. Nothing to show who this woman might have been, nothing except the conservative costume she'd been dressed in.

"Let's go to the front," said Dolly. "There's more light."

They passed through a doorway into a wide hall. Dolly led them into a room on the right—a formal sitting room, judging by the two antique settees situated at its center. A couple more mannequins stood off to one side. The gentlemen wore dark jackets with tails, beige horse-riding chaps, and tall top hats. They'd been arranged to look like they were engaged in some sort of argument, but in Claire's mind, their blank white faces made them seem like corpses. Behind them, next to the wall, was a glass case in which sat what looked like a replica of an antique revolver. If the mannequins could move, either of them would have been able to reach out and grab it. "This should do. Right?" Dolly plopped herself down on one side of a settee and crossed her legs.

"Sure," Claire answered uncertainly. She guessed that there might be all sorts of bugs and mites living in the cross-stitched fabric, but at this point, she didn't care. She and Lucas sat across from Dolly, placing Miles's bags onto the floor between them. "Should we get started?" She took out the camera and pressed the power button. There was a soft whizzing from the device, but before Claire could open the view screen, Dolly held up a hand.

"Lucas, I know you said you didn't want to talk about it, but I think you should tell us what you saw in the station." Lit by a thin beam of sunshine coming in from the window, her blond curls glowed like the dust motes floating through the still air. Part of Claire wanted to tell the girl to shush and let her check the battery. But she also understood that Lucas was dealing with something that might be just as important as watching the footage.

Lucas swallowed. "I already told you. It was Mr. Hush again."

"And what was he doing?" Dolly asked.

"He came out of the stall. He tried to pull me toward him, toward the puddle on the floor, which wasn't a puddle anymore, but a lake. A dark, deep lake. Water rose up from behind him like a wave. Like a hungry shadow. And it . . . it . . ." Lucas shuddered, then held his hands to his face, his body shuddering as he held back sobs.

Claire rested her hand on his shoulder, unsure if it was any comfort. Dolly waited for him to calm down, and when he finally looked up again, she asked, "Have you been seeing spirits for a long time?"

Lucas shook his head and wiped at his nose. "My gramma says that it's my duty to help them. They have messages they need to pass on to the living. But I don't *want* to help Mr. Hush. His message is only to hurt people. His wish is to grab whoever is closest to him and drag them down, to where he lies in his grave."

Dolly listened intently. "My mother used to see spirits. Sometimes she'd even talk to them. It was one of the reasons that we used to watch *Invisible Intelligence* together, me and her. We liked seeing how Miles handled this stuff. Before she passed away, she wrote him a letter, asking for him to come to Hush Falls and explaining the legend of the graveyard watch, and how dangerous Mr. Hush had become. She wanted Miles's help to send Hush packing. But . . . we never heard back from him. Not until he showed up with Miss Clementine at the motel. By then, it was too late for my mom." Dolly took a deep breath. "I've never met anyone else who could communicate with the dead like her."

"My gramma says it's bad to send away the spirits," Lucas answered. "She thinks that what Miles does is not a good thing. That his methods are cruel. The two of them even fought about it. For a long time."

Claire had almost forgotten this about her father and Lucas's grandmother. Sitting beside him, she felt a pang of betrayal that Lucas would share such a thing with their new friend. "We can argue about my father after we watch his footage," she said, trying to tamp down her emotions. "How about that?"

But Dolly ignored her, looking at Lucas as she went on. "But what do *you* think? Do you believe that every spirit who comes a-calling should be answered?"

"I don't . . . I don't know. Gramma thinks so. But I think . . . I think I have a lot to learn."

Dolly glanced at Claire finally. With a smile, she said, "We can help you with that. Right, Claire?"

All the tension that Claire had felt in her chest went

out the window. "Yes," she answered. "Yes, we're here for you, Lucas. Just like you were, and are, here for me."

"So then, Claire," Dolly went on, sounding like the guidance counselor at Archer's Mills Middle School, "what do you think your father would recommend Lucas do about Mr. Hush bothering him? Any advice?"

Claire hadn't considered this before. She'd been so caught up in her own fears about her missing father that she had forgotten that he was good at hunting ghosts for a reason. For many reasons. And even though Mrs. Kent didn't agree with his methods, it didn't mean that those methods were worthless. "We could . . . do some visualization to keep Mr. Hush at bay."

"Just like on the show," Lucas whispered, as if to himself.

"Right." Dolly grinned, looking pleased. "How does that go again?"

Claire closed her eyes, flipping through the scrapbook of her memory. How did her father do it? *Imagine a small orb of glowing white light. Picture it growing. Larger.*

Larger. So large that we all fit inside. Imagine that nothing else can follow us through its barrier. The light protects us from negativity, from evil, from spirits who wish us harm. When she opened her eyes again, she realized that she'd said the words aloud, because Lucas and Dolly were nodding along.

"There," said Dolly. "That didn't seem so bad, did it? Do you think your gramma would disapprove?"

Lucas sighed. "I can't see how she could." He looked to Claire. "Thank you," he said. "I already feel better. Mr. Hush won't be bothering me again anytime soon."

Dolly gave a small clap. "Perfect. Now let's get to work."

Chapter Sixteen

WHEN CLAIRE FLIPPED open the small camera's view screen, it lit up blue, showing letters and numbers around the edges that made no sense to her. There was one symbol that she did recognize, however. Examining it, she sighed in relief. The symbol showed that there was a little less than half of the battery's power left, which, Claire assumed, should be plenty to get them through what they needed to see. Or at least a good portion of it. And now that they were safe, or safer, she didn't expect any interruptions from *the beyond*. She checked that there was a tape inside, then hit rewind.

"Are you guys ready for this?" Claire asked. "It

might be difficult to watch." Lucas and Dolly nodded, but then Claire realized that she needed to ask herself the same question. What if the tape showed her something that she didn't want to see—something awful that she'd never get out of her head?

She didn't have a choice. Her father needed her, and she'd do anything to save him.

When she pressed play, Dolly came around the back of the settee and knelt down to watch the video from over Claire's shoulder.

Transcript of Miles Holiday's footage recorded in and around the town of Hush Falls Holler:

Miles Holiday—Thank you for agreeing to meet with me, Chief Bray.

Chief Bray—Happy to help, Miles. Big fan of your show!

MH—[laughing] Thank you

kindly. Now, for the purposes
of this recording, could you
please state your name and
occupation?

CB—Sure thing. Harold Bray.
Police chief of Hush Falls
Holler.

MH—And how long have you
been with the local force?

CB—About twenty-five years?
Started as a patrolman. Worked
my way up the ladder. And here
I sit today, behind the biggest
desk in the station.

MH—It suits you.

CB—I always thought it
would.

MH—Now, you already know
why I've come to Hush Falls.
Would you mind—

CB—Holler.

MH—Pardon?

CB—It's Hush Falls Holler.
[pause] Hush Falls was the
village at the bottom of the
reservoir. Doesn't quite exist
anymore, now does it?

MH—You tell me.

CB—It doesn't. The town was
moved up to these hills almost
century ago.

MH—And how long after that
did the trouble start?

CB—Oh, there have been
reports of hauntings in the
area beginning almost
immediately after the new
incorporation.

MH—And what kind of
hauntings have been reported?

CB—People talk of seeing
Lemuel Hush, one of the

descendants of the first town's founders.

MH—You sound skeptical.

CB—I've never been one for storytelling.

MH—Even as a "big fan" of my show?

CB—Well, it's one thing to watch it all from afar. It's another to have to answer to constant calls about phantom sightings from frightened town residents. I do think that people believe they've seen old Lem, but I also think that spreading these tales around can cause an unnecessary fear.

MH—Unnecessary? How then do you account for the number of drowning deaths in the reservoir over the past three-quarters of a century?

CB—People get foolish thoughts in their heads, then go out and do stupid things. They go hiking around places that are supposed to be off-limits, like the shore of that lake. Signs are posted all over that the water is meant to be protected. It feeds many of the major cities in this state. There aren't proper trails. The ground is tricky. Things happen!

MH—How many have died on your watch?

CB—My watch? What are you insinuating?

MH—What I mean is, since you've been with the force, how many times have you had to investigate a death for which people said Lemuel Hush was responsible?

CB—[sighing] I don't know all of what people say around here. But if you're asking how many have drowned in the past twenty-five years, I'd wager it would probably be close to . . . thirteen people? Which, in my opinion, is minuscule compared to the number our country lost to the waves.

MH—Every death matters, no? Just like every life?

CB—When you imagine the sheer number. The loss . . . It's hard to think about it in those terms, but . . . of course. Of course.

MH—And were those thirteen

victims members of this community?

CB—Some. Not all.

MH—Can you tell me about any of them?

CB—Now, Mr. Holiday, you have to understand that these are private matters—

MH—I don't need names. But any insight you could give into the circumstances . . .

CB—[after a moment] The first I remember was a couple of young brothers. They'd gone out to the reservoir to fish. People used to do that all the time around here till the state cracked down. There was good fishing in that lake. Anyway, the older of the two came running home and told his

mother that a man had strolled
up out of the shallows,
picked up the younger brother,
and carried him screaming back
into the water. We went out and
searched the area. [pause] We
found the child's body. Not a
sight you want lodged in your
dreams, I'll tell you that much.
The parents never believed the
older kid's story. Said he was
making it up so that he
wouldn't feel responsible. Or
something. That family didn't
stick around town much longer.
In fact, lots of folks moved
away after that.

　　MH—Horrible. I'm so sorry.

　　CB—Most of the other stories
go just like that. The most
recent, however, was a woman, a

young mother, who'd got it into

her head—

Claire clicked the pause button. "Maybe we should skip over this part." She glanced at Dolly, who was suddenly pale.

"Good idea," Dolly whispered.

Lucas nodded sadly.

Claire zoomed the video forward until the background changed and a different face appeared on the screen—a middle-aged woman wearing a brown-and-orange diner uniform. She stood just behind a silver-rimmed Formica counter. Dozens of drinking glasses lined the silver shelves behind her.

"Oh, I know her," said Dolly. "She's—"

But then the video began to play.

Miles Holiday—Please state

your name and your occupation.

Candace Watkins—Well, my

name's just as it says here on

my tag. Candace. And I'm a
waitress here at the Holler
Diner.

MH—How long have you lived
in Hush Falls Holler?

CW—All my life. Which would
be twenty-nine years and not a
day older. But don't you go
asking anyone else if that's
true or not. [chuckling]
I wouldn't wanna have to
give any of my coworkers a
black eye!

MH—You say you have a Lemuel
Hush story, Candace. Would you
mind sharing it?

CW—I'm not saying I don't
mind. But I will share it.
It was a few years back after
a late shift here at the diner.
My buddy Sharon Pickul asks me

if I'd mind giving her a ride
home, since her husband is
still at work and can't pick
her up. So I say, sure thing,
hon. And off we go. Now, Sharon
lives out on one of those
unpaved roads over near the
old quarry. Full of potholes,
size of prizewinning
watermelons. I hate going that
way because you have to drive
like this. [imitates holding a
steering wheel and swinging it
sharply left and right]

Anyway, I get Sharon home
and she waves goodbye and I'm
off again in my little sedan so
I can get home myself. Now,
part of that road skirts kinda
close to the reservoir . . . Of
course, I've heard the stories

of Lemuel Hush. Everybody in the Holler has. But I ain't never seen him myself. Till that night. Hoo-boy. [shivers]

My headlights are peeping through the darkness, and I'm going real slow so I don't take off one of my tires, when all of a sudden there's someone standing in the middle of the road. A man. Right in front of my car. And I swerve to avoid him but I hit one of them potholes and wouldn't you know I'm off the road and barreling through the forest like a deer being chased by a great big grizzly. I was so scared I don't remember putting my foot on the brake or nothing. I'm just holding on to that wheel trying not to steer myself into a dang tree. And the last thing I remember is seeing that same man step out of the shadows into my high beams. And he was smiling. This awful, awful smile. Like a shark. Or no . . . a barracuda! Big fish. Giant mouth. Lots of teeth. I swear, I drove right through him.

I hear this horrible sound, like someone wrenching the earth apart. And then there's dark. When I come to, I see the sun rising over the lake and I think to myself, how gorgeous. But then I get to wondering how it is I'm waking up at the lake and I look around and realize that I'm not just at the lake. I'm in the lake! I'd somehow crash-landed right into the reservoir. I'd been there all night long.

There's this gash on my head and dried blood on my face. I try to start up my car, but the engine won't turn over. So, I open the door and step out into the water. It's up to here on me. [indicates her upper-mid calf] And I crawl up onto the shore and I turn around and see the state of things and then realize what had happened. If my car had been going any faster, I might have driven deeper into the water. I might have . . . Well, I don't like to think about it. So, I run through the woods to the road up to Sharon's house and tell

her the problem and we call
the police and a tow truck
comes for my car and let me
tell you, I ain't never been
back to Sharon's house and I
also ain't never been back to
that lake because I know what
Old Hush was trying to do to
me, steal me down to his
sunken graveyard, likely, down
there at the bottom, and I
don't want to take my chances a
second time. No, sir, I do not.

The clip cut out, and a new face appeared—a man dressed in a blue plaid cotton button-down. He was standing in a room that was similar to the one in which the three were sitting. Claire looked closer and noticed the two faceless mannequins standing just off to the side of the man, who was staring into the camera. It wasn't just similar; it *was* the same room.

Reed Winterson—How do
I look?

Miles Holiday—Like a million
dollars. Could you please
introduce yourself?

RW—You already know who I
am, Mr. Holiday. Everyone
around here does.

MH—It's just so we can
have a log of it for my
production team.

RW—Well sure, then I'll say
it again for the production
team. [with a big smile] I'm
Reed Winterson. And I'm the
mayor of Hush Falls Hollow.

MH—Is it Hollow or Holler?

RW—It is whatever you want it
to be. We don't discriminate here.

MH—How long have you been
the mayor?

RW—Going on fifteen years.

MH—That's a long time! You
must have seen the town
through quite a few changes.

RW—Oh, certainly. Certainly.
Every community has its share
of ups and downs.

MH—You must admit though
that Hush Falls Holler stands
out from other local
communities in a very big way.

RW—[laughs] Of course, I'll
admit that. It's why you've
decided to visit us, is it not?

MH—You believe the stories
people tell?

RW—It doesn't really matter
what I believe. What matters
is what I'm willing to do about it.

MH—And what would that be?

RW—To make Hush Falls Hollow
as appealing as possible. To
bring us the attention we
deserve as a historic site, as
a scenic destination, and yes,
as a place that people are
hungry to visit.

MH—Do you believe that it is
still a safe place at this
point?

RW—Safer than the cities and
towns along the coast. The
ones that are still standing,
that is. We have so much to
offer. I've been working with
the chamber of commerce to
build up business, and inch by
inch, we are beginning to grow.
We aren't only the spooky
stories that people tell about

us. Our citizens are warm, friendly, hardworking. We have a whole lot to offer.

MH—Like this building? Your museum.

RW—[nodding] It is our goal to fix up the Hush Falls Museum by the end of the year. It was quite a feat moving an entire town into the hills. Something we can be proud of as uniquely our own.

MH—Are you looking to reopen some of your own business efforts that have fallen by the wayside?

RW—None of them have "fallen by the wayside." I like to think of them more as "seasonal closures." And I'd like to believe they'll be back in business in no time. I am very jobs-oriented. I care deeply about the welfare of my constituents. Work is important to them.

MH—Some might say that the spirit of Lemuel Hush could be a big lure for tourists looking for a glimpse of the supernatural.

RW—[shaking his head] I'd never actively take advantage of anyone's tragedy. And yes, I will admit that over the years, this area has had its fair share of misfortune. But I'd say no. Hush Falls Hollow would never rely on old Lem—may he rest in peace—to help increase our property values. [chuckling] That's just not the way we

think around here, Mr. Holiday.
However, I promise you this,
just as I promised voters
during the last town election:
Our time is coming. We will
rise again. And we plan on
doing it the right way.

Again, the video cut to a new scene. Now, instead of the camera perched steadily in front of a talking head, the image on the view screen was moving through a heavily wooded area.

Miles Holiday—Since
Clementine is still finishing
up her own interviews with
some of the other townsfolk,
I figured I'd explore the area
near where Candace Watkins
claimed to have seen Lemuel Hush
right before she crashed her

car. You can see here by the
side of the road where some of
the smaller trees were taken
out, their trunks sheared off
several inches above the
roots. And these lower branches
on the nearby trees are broken
as well.

[Image—The forest floor.
Several broken saplings lie
rotting on the ground. The
camera moves toward the trees
on either side, revealing
places where their branches
were snapped off. The image
lingers for several seconds
before moving farther down the
hill, away from the road.]

MH—Clem and I will come
back together out here later,
to gather a few establishing

shots, and I'll do some further
narration. But for now . . . I'll
explore on my own.

[Image—The camera points
directly down the hill. The
lake appears vaguely through
the pine branches and scrub
brush.]

MH—I believe I'm standing on
the north side of the water.
Somewhere nearby is the mouth
of the Black Ribbon River,
which feeds the reservoir. If
you listen closely, you can
just barely make it out.
Whispering. Babbling. Do you
hear that? It almost sounds
like voices calling for help.

"I don't like this," said Claire. "He's out there by
himself. Right where that waitress was attacked."

"But this might be the most important part," Dolly answered.

"Do you want me to hold the camera?" Lucas asked. Claire fought the urge to hand it over. "No. I got it."

```
MH—[walking, slightly out of
breath] Yes, I think this would
be a perfect place for some
narration. We could join pieces
of Candace's story with these
images. Maybe even find a way
to reconstruct her descent
down this slope into the water.
```

"He sounds so confident," stated Dolly. "No fear at all."

"Maybe he didn't believe Candace's story?" Lucas considered.

"My father's a brave man," said Claire. "He must have known what he was doing . . . Or at least he *thought* he did."

[Image—The trees break apart as the camera nears the shoreline. The sky is revealed, reflecting a bright blue on the calm surface of the water below.]

MH—Almost looks like a mirror. How lovely. [pausing] It was probably right about here where Candace landed.

[Image—The camera focuses on the water several yards away from the shore. Lake grasses poke through the surface like needles.]

MH—What the . . .

[Image—The camera moves upward swiftly, then concentrates farther out on the water. Impossibly, there appears to be a figure

standing on the surface.
He stares directly at the
camera.]

MH—[stammering, flustered]
Is that . . . What am I seeing
here? I—I can't . . . Could it
be . . . Is that Lemuel Hush?

[Image—Stabilizes on the
figure. A man. Dressed in gray
pants, black boots, and a thick
overcoat with a burst of black
fur at the collar. Dark hair
slicked into a severe part at
the side of his head. His eyes
dark, hidden in pockets of
shadow, his mouth a deep
straight gash carved just below
his long nose.]

MH—[calmer, but still
excitable] If what I'm seeing
here is actually captured on

this recording, I may finally
have rare visual proof of a
supernatural occurrence. Layne,
are you seeing this? [laughs]
How much would you be willing
to cough up for this exclusive?
[pause. In awe] This is
incredible. I can't—

    [Image—The figure drops
quickly down into the surface
of the water. Ripples spread
outward from the spot, like a
bull's-eye.]

Claire gasped. Lucas reached out to steady the camera so they could all keep watching.

    MH—Where'd he go? [pause,
then fearfully] What the . . .
    [Image—The ripples are
coming toward the camera. The

water bulges and a wake forms.
Whatever is moving under the
surface is moving lightning
fast and heading directly for
Miles. The camera drops down
as Miles stumbles backward.
We are looking at a pair of
boots. He grunts, then takes
off running up the hill.
The camera sways back and
forth. A blur of mud and dirt
and brush for several seconds
as Miles struggles for
breath.]

MH—[shouting] Help! Help me!
Somebody!

[Sound—A great walloping
thump.]

[Image—The camera falls into
the brush. It lies there for
several seconds, focusing and

refocusing on the grasses in
its immediate range.]

[Sound—Footsteps.]

[Image—Large black boots
stop in front of the lens. A
shadow blocks the sunlight. The
screen goes dark.]

The tape stopped, and the view screen turned blue.

Claire's entire body felt numb. Lucas took the camera from her as she felt herself go limp. Dolly came around the couch and crouched in front of her. "Claire?" she said. "Claire. Look at me."

But Claire didn't want to look at anything. She wanted to stop breathing. She wanted to close her eyes and float away. To dream. To be among the stars. To fight a battle against alien hordes. Anything. *Anything* to keep herself from thinking of what she had just seen. What the camera had shown her.

"He's out there," she heard herself say. "He's out at that lake. Near where Candace crashed her car." She sat up, felt herself rush back into her body. Here was an answer. A clue! "That's where he fell. That's where he must be!" She tried to stand, but Dolly grasped her hands.

"Claire, you look kind of green. Maybe don't get up just yet."

Rrrrrck! The floor creaked. The sound echoed into the sitting room from out in the wide hall. All three of them turned to look.

But there was just another one of those mannequins stationed in the room across the way.

Its blackish eyes looked back at Claire, and a jangling sensation twanged her nerves. She glanced at the figures in the sitting room, observing, with a sharp breath, their blank white faces. The mannequins did not have blackish eyes. Claire stood, nearly dropping the camera from her lap as Lucas caught it. Her body felt light. Tingly. She turned back to the doorway, not quite wanting to see what was there.

"Do you guys see him?" Lucas whispered.

"Yes," both girls answered.

The figure across the hallway came into clearer focus. Claire recognized now that its clothes were not old-fashioned. A puffy beige coat. Blue jeans. Muddy running shoes.

This was no mannequin.

Chapter Seventeen

A THOUGHT FLASHED at Claire—a memory of a conversation with her father from a year or so back. He'd sat her down in his office and showed her a photograph of a man's face. Round cheeks. A small, puckered mouth. Piercing eyes. Prominent ears. And a head full of thick blond hair. Her father had explained who he was: Tanner Worley. A fan of *Invisible Intelligence* who had taken his interest in the show a little too seriously. Tanner had been showing up at the production offices, asking to see Miles, asking about future episodes of the show, asking for a job. They had told him to stay away, but then he had appeared in Archer's Mills, and Miles had called the police. Miles had made Claire memorize the picture so she'd know who to look out for in case the man ever showed up.

And here he was. In Hush Falls Holler.

"Tanner?" Claire whispered.

The man's eyes went wide. He turned and disappeared around the edge of the doorway. "Tanner!" she called out, dashing to the hall. The door at the back of the house squealed open then slammed shut. "Come on," she said to the others before taking off.

"Who was that guy?" Dolly asked.

Claire bolted to the kitchen. Only when she opened the rear door did she wonder if chasing after her father's stalker was a great idea. But now, Tanner was nowhere to be seen. She came to the edge of the screened porch and listened for a clue of which way he'd gone. There was only the hushed whisper of a breeze through the grass.

"A man was just watching us," said Lucas, out of breath, "and you *know* him?"

Claire nodded.

"I'm confused," said Dolly. "Is he a friend? Of your family?"

"No. Not a friend." Claire told them about Tanner. About how the law had to get involved. About the restraining order.

"Your dad has a stalker?" Dolly asked, aghast.

"I didn't recognize him at first. Mostly because I didn't expect to see him. It's been a while."

"Why would he be here?" Lucas asked.

"He must have been following my dad." Claire allowed her eyes to flit around the backyard.

Lucas sniffed. "Following? Or maybe . . . Do you think *he* could be the reason your dad is missing?"

"Maybe he saw us around town and tracked us to the museum. When I went after him, I was thinking we could talk to him, find out what he's seen, what he knows." Or what he's *done*, she thought.

"Should we go tell the police?" asked Dolly.

Lucas shook his head. "Wouldn't we have to tell

them that *we're* here too? They'd send us home right away."

"But if this Tanner person is responsible for"—Dolly sighed—"for whatever happened to Claire's dad, maybe it's dangerous for you two to be here at all."

"I'm not going home without my father," Claire said simply. "Especially now that we know that Tanner Worley has been watching."

"Maybe Dolly could ask around," said Lucas. "We could find out where Tanner's staying."

Dolly crossed her arms. "The only place to stay is at my grandparents' motel and I can already tell you he's not there. The last people to check in were Miles and Clementine."

"Maybe we could call in an anonymous tip. Let the police track Tanner. Question him themselves. He can't be far."

"That's a good idea," said Claire. "At least he's gone for now." She shuddered. "And we have to get to the lake. To that spot where my father's footage cut out. Dolly, can you show us the way?"

Dolly held her hand to her forehead. "It's a really bad place, Claire. And the police said they already searched that area, didn't they?"

Claire shook herself out. "Okay then, I can go by myself."

"No, you can't," said Lucas. "What if we're in over our heads? Maybe . . . maybe this isn't a job for us anymore."

"My mother wouldn't have asked me to come if she thought I couldn't do it."

"I don't think your mother was thinking about that part. When she came knocking, I heard only desperation. She was scared for your father. And if she were here right now, I bet she'd only want us to leave."

"How could you say that to me?" Claire asked. "After all that we've been through today?"

"I'll show you the way," Dolly answered, looking resigned. "It's a bit of a hike. I bet we could get there before sunset if we start now. We can leave your dad's bags here. They'll be too heavy to carry."

"Thank you, *Dolly*." Claire said her name a little too hard. Lucas flinched.

"This way," said Dolly, leading them down the steps to the yard, heading around the side of the house, where a thin alley was marked by the house's wall and a row of bushy evergreens. Following it would take them to the street. "What I want to know is: If your dad's camera fell into the leaves out in the woods by the lake, how did it end up at the police station?"

Claire felt herself pale. "Do you think someone at the station is involved?"

"Could Tanner have brought it to them?" asked Lucas.

Dolly shrugged. "Maybe? Unless the police found it during the search of the shoreline—" She stopped short. Ahead, a shadow was blocking their path. Someone was standing at the end of the alley.

Claire grabbed at Lucas's and Dolly's hands, ready to pull them in the opposite direction, away from Tanner. But then a voice called out. "Lucas Kent! Don't you move!"

The words stopped Claire short. She looked back

and realized who had discovered them, almost wishing that it *had* been Tanner Worley. Because now Lucas's grandmother, Irene, was staring them down, and she looked the opposite of happy to see them.

Chapter Eighteen

"GRAMMA?" LUCAS'S VOICE was as soft as a mouse scurrying along the gravel path. "What are you doing here?"

"What am *I* doing here? You're really going to ask me that question?" Irene fumed. "I came to get you and bring you back to Archer's Mills. You and Claire." She considered Dolly. "I don't know you, but I'll be sure *you* get home as well."

"We don't want to go home, Mrs. Kent," Claire answered.

"I don't care what you want, young lady. What you two have done today is beyond comprehension. I got a message from your school while I was at the salon that Lucas never came to homeroom this morning. And after our conversation last night, I immediately had my suspicions. I checked with Claire's aunt, Lizzie. She got the same call that I did. I packed up my pickup and hit the road."

"But how did you know we were here exactly?" asked Dolly, looking more enthralled than frightened. She was in awe of Irene.

"When I reached the town, I felt something pulling at me. A white-light visualization. I followed the sensation to this building. And here you are."

Lucas composed himself, trying to sound rational. "Gramma, we're sorry for running off and not telling you. But last night, Claire's mom visited me again. She wouldn't leave me alone. It was like she was creeping through my brain. She said that she wouldn't stop unless we did this."

Irene looked horrified. "You should have told me. I could have stopped her."

"But I don't want to stop her," Lucas said. "I want

to help Claire. We're close, I think. Since we've come to town, we've learned a whole lot. We even have an idea of where to explore next."

Irene looked ready to explode. But after a moment, her face changed. It was like she was seeing them for the first time. She sighed. "You three must be starving. I passed a diner about a block away. Come on. Let's go eat."

She took Lucas's hand and led him out of the alley-way. He was torn. Part of him wished that his gramma would just put her foot down and take them away from this place. The other part wanted to finish what he had started. But all of him was hungry.

At the diner, they piled into a booth in the back corner. Lucas didn't see Candace, the waitress who Miles had interviewed. A different woman brought them menus.

Dolly introduced herself to Irene, explaining that she lived at the motel. She told Irene that when Claire and Lucas had arrived and explained their situation, she had felt compelled to help them. She explained about her mother's drowning and about the legend of the graveyard watch. She told her about Lemuel Hush and about her mother's idea that he was looking for a replacement, so that his soul would be freed from the graveyard and he could finally pass on.

Claire mentioned gathering Miles's things from the police station, which Irene took in with a raised eyebrow. Lucas described viewing the footage in the sitting room of the Hush Falls Museum, including where the tape had cut off. He also explained how he'd been seeing Lemuel Hush, and how Mr. Hush was sending him frightening visions of floods. Claire finished with the tale of discovering Tanner Worley, her father's stalker, watching them from across the hall.

"And where is this man now?" asked Irene. "Tanner?"

"We're not sure," said Claire. "We were thinking of calling in a tip to the police to let them know he's in town. We don't know how he's involved. If he hurt my dad. Or if he knows anything about where he is."

"I cannot believe this," Irene said as if to herself. "You kids . . ." She just shook her head again. "I was never this brave when I was your age."

That was not what Lucas had thought she was going to say. He felt proud of himself, and wondered if, maybe only slightly, she was proud of him too.

"You see, Mrs. Kent?" Claire went on. "We can't go back to Archer's Mills. Not just yet. We're close. My father . . . I can feel him. Can't you?"

"I feel a lot of things in this place. It's all very . . . overwhelming." Irene reached across the table and took Lucas's hand. "You're all right? Mr. Hush didn't hurt you?"

"No, Gramma. He didn't. And Claire's visualization helped."

"Those things don't last forever. We still need to keep an eye out."

"So, we can stay?" Claire jumped in her seat. "You'll help me find my father?"

Irene rolled her eyes, then closed them for what felt like a long while. "I will," she said. When she looked at Lucas again, she shot him a glare. "But don't think I'm just going to let this go. When we get home, you are grounded. Do you understand?" Lucas nodded, totally fine with that. She turned to Claire. "I agree that these police are not to be trusted. It's strange that they had Miles's camera. We'll hold off on contacting them for now."

The waitress stopped by and they ordered lunch. Burgers and fries and mozzarella sticks and milkshakes and nachos. Everything comforting that they could find on the menu. They needed it.

Chapter Nineteen

AFTER THEY WERE finished eating, they climbed into Irene's giant pickup truck, and Dolly gave directions toward the road where Sharon Pickul lived, which would bring them to where Miles had been exploring the lakeshore.

The waitress from the interview had been right—the road was a mess. Irene drove slowly, but even so, the truck lurched left and right as its tires drove over the many potholes and divots where rainwater had washed the gravel away. "Here!" Claire shouted as they came to a bend. "I recognize this area from the video camera. This is where my father began taping that last part." Irene slowed to a halt, then pulled over.

As they walked down the hill, Lucas glanced all around. He couldn't get what his gramma had said out of his head—that Claire's white-light protection would not last. He hated to think of Lemuel Hush appearing again, but then he remembered that he was not alone in this anymore. If he were to see Lemuel, then surely Gramma would as well. And if she was as fearsome to Lemuel as she was to Lucas, then maybe, just maybe, everything would be okay.

"Oh, this is odd," Irene said, stomping through the brush. "I feel very strange indeed."

"Strange in what way, Gramma?"

"Ever since I came into the town, I thought it was odd that I could feel no presence of spirits. Nothing. It was very unusual." She held her hand above her eyes, blocking out the light. "But here, I can feel a dozen or more, the people I sensed last night while gazing into the milk and ink. Their spirits linger. Trapped. Lemuel Hush is the one keeping them here."

"You can feel *all that*?" Dolly asked in wonder.

Irene smiled. "I've had many years to learn." She glanced at Lucas with a knowing glint in her eye, as if to say, *You, my boy, are just beginning.*

"Do you . . ." Dolly began. "Do you feel the spirit of my mother? Her name's Missy Snedecker."

Irene squinted. Then she nodded. "I do."

"My mother is *here*? Is there anything you can do to help her?"

"I will certainly try," Irene said, smiling. Lucas could tell she was forcing it, and he felt suddenly horrible for Dolly. For all that she had been through.

The path down the slope was just how it had been on the tape. The trees were dense and tall. The pines wore enough foliage to spread sporadic shadows across the forest floor.

Then it appeared. The lake.

The sun was too far behind them at this point to cast any real light upon it, but still, it seemed to glow, reflecting the endless blue expanse overhead. They came through the brush to the shore. The grass was high there. Lucas listened to the wind through the distant forest. Under any other circumstance, it might have been calming.

Things were different since the waves had taken the coast. Lucas could still remember a time when everything had been filled with sound. Highways humming constantly somewhere over a horizon. Airplanes droning across the great blue. People chatting on their handheld devices. Now the world was quieter. And up here, in Hush Falls Holler, when the wind stopped blowing, the silence made him feel like they were some of the only people left. In a way—in several ways—they were.

"Do you still sense her?" Dolly asked. "My mother?"

"I did," said Irene. "But now she may be hiding. With all the others."

"This is where it happened," said Claire. "Where my father saw Lemuel Hush hovering out on the water. There is where he ran. And farther, where he dropped his camera."

"He's not here anymore," said Lucas.

"Obviously," Claire answered sharply, and he winced. "Sorry, Lucas. I don't know what I thought we would find here." She stared out at the lake. A pine-covered island rose from the water—a bunch of bristles, about five hundred yards from the shore. The lake continued beyond it for a great distance. This reservoir was enormous. It went on for miles. "I feel so . . . stupid."

"Gramma, what do you see?"

"The same as you, Lucas. Water. Trees. The sky. Birds."

A voice came from behind them. "*I* saw something."

All of them turned. Lucas stumbled, almost tumbling into the damp sand by the water's edge. A man was standing between the trees up the hill, a dozen feet away. Lucas recognized him immediately.

Chapter Twenty

IRENE HELD OUT her arms to the kids, and they gathered close. "And you are?" she asked the man. His blond hair fell over his forehead and almost covered his eyes. His cheeks were flushed, as if he had run here.

"I'm Tanner, ma'am. Tanner Worley."

Claire whispered, "He's the one who was watching us. The one my father warned me about."

"I'm sorry if I scared you. I saw you kids at the museum earlier and, well, I guess you could say I followed you out here."

"For what purpose?" Irene answered harshly.

"I wanted to . . . to talk to you."

"You're not allowed to talk to us," said Claire, her voice rising. "My father has an order against you."

Tanner's gaze fell. "I know. I should've kept my distance from him. But I got word of where he was scouting. And when I found out it was to be Hush Falls Holler, I just couldn't stay away. I've been sleeping in my car, parked behind one of the abandoned cottages just off the highway."

"So, you didn't do anything to Miles?" Lucas asked.

Tanner looked gut-punched. "Me? Of course not! I would never. I've only ever just been a fan."

"A fan who wouldn't leave us alone," said Claire, her eyes slivered. "A fan who showed up at our house."

"I was just as shocked to learn that Miles had gone missing as the rest of you."

"Then you didn't follow him out here?" asked Dolly. "Like you followed us?"

"No, no. At that time, I was sitting at the diner. Listening to Clementine interview a couple people who had ghost stories to tell. If I'd known he was in trouble I would have helped him. I swear."

"So, what did you see?" Claire asked.

"Pardon me?" answered the man.

"You said you saw something here. What was it?"

Tanner shuddered. He came down to the water's edge and trod through the tall grass. The group moved away from him. "This place is spookier than most of the other locations that *Invisible Intelligence* has explored. You can feel it in the air. Can't you?" He ran his hand through his hair. Then he pointed to the island—the one that looked like brush bristles rising from the water's surface. "It was out there. Last night. I was down the shore maybe a mile. But I could still see it. A light. Flickering slightly. But surely. It looked like a campfire."

Claire spun to gaze out over the water. Lucas had to grab her wrist to keep her from soaking her sneakers. "Daddy?" she whispered to herself. Then she turned to Irene, a wild look in her eyes. "He's out there! Dad! Daddy!" she called. Her voice resounded across the water. "It's me! Claire! We're coming to get you!"

Irene held out her arm, directing the kids back onto

the shore. "If Miles is the one on the island with the light, how did he get there?"

"No idea," said Tanner, stepping deeper into the grasses, as if mesmerized. The water rippled at his feet. "I went to the police. I told them what I saw. Then I waited. As far as I know, no one's followed up. Maybe they decided I was a kook. But you'd think they'd at least check. When they didn't, I spent the rest of the morning trying to track down a boat so I could row out there myself. But no one would lend me one. Something about the water being protected. Boats aren't allowed."

"Sure they are," said Dolly, shaking her head. "You just have to clean them properly before you put them in and then again after you take them out. Whoever told you that was lying." She looked fearful. "Do you remember who it was?"

Tanner sighed. "I don't."

She turned to the others. "We have a couple of canoes behind the motel. Paddles and everything. They might even fit in the back of your truck, Mrs. Kent."

Claire lit up. "Let's go get them!"

"Hold up, hold *up!*" said Irene. "We can't just go rowing out across the reservoir by ourselves."

"Why not, Gramma?"

She threw her hands into the air. "We don't even have life jack—"

Something splashed at the water, rustling the grass where Tanner was standing. Before Lucas could think to move away, Tanner's feet went out from under him. He flew onto his back, landing with a splat and a splash. He went sliding into the water, as if something was dragging him. "Help!" Tanner cried out.

He grabbed on to big clumps of grass, trying to hold himself in place. Turning over, he looked to the group. His marble-like eyes bulged with terror. His knuckles were white where he clutched at the grass. Their roots were coming up, making Tanner slide deeper into the lake.

"Something has me! Please! Pull me out!"

Chapter Twenty-One

IRENE STUMBLED AFTER Tanner, reaching for his hands. But before she could catch him, the grass roots let go, and Tanner disappeared into the shallows with a distinct *shloop!*

"It's Lemuel," Lucas cried. "I can feel him here. He's . . . he's trying to take another victim."

"Stand back," Irene shouted. "All of you. Far back. Near the trees!" Lucas, Claire, and Dolly all did what she said.

Several feet out, Tanner thrashed his body, splashing lake water up into the air. But Lem was keeping him under, drowning the man. The ghost was invisible, but he was clearly there.

The kids clutched one another, watching as Irene raised her arms over her head. She was whispering something to herself. Tanner was slowing. Losing energy. Dipping below the surface. Irene stomped her feet, then held her hands out toward the water, imploringly.

To Lucas's surprise, the water bulged where Tanner was struggling. Then, impossibly, its surface began to spin. The spinning spread out and down, just like the whirlpools that would form over the drain whenever Lucas would let water out of the kitchen sink.

The water's surface dipped, and Tanner was able to raise his head up just enough to catch a breath before being yanked down again.

Claire grabbed at Lucas's and Dolly's jacket sleeves. "You guys remember the white orb I mentioned earlier? The one my father taught me to visualize?"

"Of course," said Dolly. Lucas nodded.

"Picture it with me now. Okay?" Claire closed her eyes. "White light. Growing larger."

Lucas and Dolly closed their eyes too. Lucas imagined the orb floating before him.

"Larger," Claire continued. "Larger still. Now . . . send it out to Tanner. Imagine it helping us. Helping *him*."

Lucas opened his eyes. In his mind, the orb dipped down and enclosed Tanner inside it.

Something was happening out on the water. The whirlpool was widening. The bottom of the lake was revealed.

Claire spoke. "Protect us from negativity, from spirits who wish us harm." Tanner was on all fours on the cleared muddy bottom of the lake, his torso heaving as he tried to catch his breath. Between their visualizing, and whatever Irene was doing to the water, it was working. The group was forcing Lemuel Hush away.

"Over here!" Irene called to Tanner.

Looking confused and terrified, the man got to his feet. Tanner made eye contact with her, and suddenly, a determined expression came over him. He stumbled forward, the whirlpool following him up the embank-ment, until he was standing safely again on the shore. The opening in the water splashed closed again, sending small shivers out into the lake.

Irene raced over to Tanner and caught him before he could collapse. "Lucas, a little help!" Lucas ran to them and assisted his gramma as she heaved the man up toward the woods. They placed Tanner at the base of a pine trunk, where he slumped and put his head between his knees.

"Are you okay, mister?" Dolly asked, rushing to join them.

Tanner could only groan.

"What was that, Gramma?" Lucas asked. "That whirlpool thing? Where did it come from?"

Sweat beaded on Irene's forehead. "I asked the spirits trapped in the lake to help us. They were able to move the water just so. That, along with what you three were doing, kept Lemuel Hush at bay."

Tanner's head flicked upward. His eyes widened as he stared out at the water. He scrambled to his feet, holding the tree trunk for support. "I can't . . . I can't be here." He turned and began to hike up the slope toward the dirt road.

"Where do you think you're going?" Irene asked him.

"Home," said the man. His wet clothes clung to him and he shivered. "This was a mistake. A big, big mistake."

"What about Miles?" asked Lucas. "Don't you want to help him?"

Tanner spun on him. "And how would I do that? You four think you're gonna hop in some canoes and head out to that island? It's a death wish. Call the police. Tell them what I told you."

"You said you already called the police," Dolly spat. "They didn't do anything."

Tanner was quiet for a moment. Then he headed up the hill again. "This isn't my problem," he said over his shoulder.

Claire started to race toward him, but Irene placed her hand on the back of Claire's neck. "Let him go," she said quietly. Lucas and Dolly stood by and watched

Tanner disappear between the trees. His footsteps crunched through the brush for a while longer. Then, except for some birdsong and the rush of the wind, the world was quiet again.

~ PART THREE ~

THE SILENCE

Chapter Twenty-Two

THEY KNEW WHAT they needed to do. They didn't even discuss it.

When they reached Irene's truck, they climbed inside. Dolly directed them back toward the main road, and from there Irene was able to locate the Lost Village Motor Lodge. The canoes were behind the long building, right where Dolly had said they would be.

Claire worried that Dolly's family would come out and confront them, but no one appeared.

The sun was low in the sky now. Shadows of the pines stretched wide across the parking lot. The atmosphere took on an amber hue, and the light around them seemed to glow.

The four worked together to get the two boats into the back of the pickup. "Do we need to wash these down first?" asked Claire.

Dolly smiled sadly, adding four oars to the truck's bed. "I think we can make an exception this one time."

As Irene was pulling out onto the road a few minutes later, Claire was suddenly overcome with relief. "We're really doing this," she said, trying to control the shimmer in her voice. "We're going to rescue my father." She didn't know how to feel when the others did not answer. Maybe they were thinking of what they'd seen happen to Tanner Worley, or maybe their understanding of the situation was so solid they felt no need to agree aloud.

Dolly pointed the way toward a service road that would get them most quickly to the shore. Irene drove up as close to the water as she could get, which turned out to be about twenty feet away, and then they unloaded the canoes. This was farther from the island than the spot where Miles's tape had cut off, but they all knew they couldn't go back there again. Toward the northern end of the lake, the bristle pine island seemed to float quietly. Waiting for them.

"Stay away from the water for now," said Irene. "At least until we can prepare ourselves."

Moments later, Claire talked Lucas and Dolly into the protective white orb.

"I really feel like I should go out there alone," Irene stated.

Lucas shook his head. "Penelope said that Claire needed to come. She said she needed my help too. We have to go with you."

"Dolly?" Irene asked. "Maybe you should stay here? Keep watch?"

"Watch for what?" asked Dolly. "I'm sorry, Mrs. Kent. But you said my mother's spirit is here in this water. If there's a way I can connect with her this evening, I'm going to do it." She steadied her chin. "I'm going to rescue her too."

"You realize what that may entail?" Dolly looked confused, and Irene went on. "Not only are we trying to save Claire's father, but we'll need to banish Lemuel Hush entirely."

"Gramma," Lucas whispered. "I thought you didn't believe in doing stuff like that?"

"I've never encountered something so dangerous. Most of my spirits have only ever needed guidance. Or to pass along a message to the living. But not Lemuel. Graveyard watch or not, he cannot remain in Hush Falls . . . or in the Holler."

"But how?" asked Claire. "How do we *banish* him?"

Irene's eyes flickered across the landscape, worried. "I'd rather not say." Then she whispered, "Not out loud."

The sky was dimming. A shadow of its former glorious blue was mirrored in the glassy surface of the reservoir. It was difficult for Claire to imagine that an entire town had once stood here—that parts of the community still remained below, hidden in a world of reflected light, reflected reality, like a ghost itself.

Irene gathered two flashlights from her truck. She gave the signal, and the group slid the canoes across the sandy slope and down into the water. Claire climbed into one of the boats with Lucas. He grabbed hold of the oars. Irene went with Dolly, steering their own little vessel.

Slowly, slowly they moved away from the shore. In her mind, Claire thought of the white light again, thankful for her father's methods, thankful that he was probably using them himself wherever he was. She knew that Miles and Irene did not agree about how to handle the dead. But now, both of their ideas were working together, as if they had always been meant to do so.

Crossing the water, no one felt the need to talk. Claire was grateful for it. All she could think about was the look she'd see in her father's face when they came up onto the far shore and she could throw her arms around him.

When they were out in the middle of the lake, canoes gliding together only several feet apart, Claire paused in her silent meditation and noticed a light flickering low in the trees. It was exactly as Tanner Worley had said it would be. A faded, pulsing orange. A campfire, or maybe a lantern. Whatever it was, it meant they were moving in the right direction. Toward her father. Toward an answer. A few stars began to appear in the sky overhead as well as below, and as daylight continued to fade away, more and more of them came into view. Claire thought back to yesterday—had it only been yesterday?—when she'd noticed the stars outside her bedroom window, back in Archer's Mills. How they'd blinked at her, made it seem as though her mother was standing behind her, signaling her. Maybe Claire didn't have sight in the same way that Lucas and Irene did, but this quick memory gave her hope that maybe every person could sense lost loved ones now and again, even if it was only a trick of light.

Dolly gasped. She leaned over the side of the boat, looking down. "What's this?" she said, pointing. Everyone paused and peered carefully into the darkening water. Below, Claire noticed movement. She braced herself for an attack from Lemuel and focused on the white orb.

Several feet below the surface, gauzy shapes were gliding through the water. They were glowing from within, emitting their own light, like jellyfish or octopuses. But these shapes were larger and longer than those animals. As Claire stared, she made out a face gazing up at her. She jolted back, knocking the boat so that it rocked, spilling water inside. "Those are people!" she cried out.

"Shh," said Irene. "We don't want to scare them."

"Scare them?" Lucas asked. "What about them scaring us?"

"We know what they are. And we also know by now that *these* spirits are nothing to be frightened of."

"Do I *really* know that, Gramma?" Lucas grimaced.

"Mama!" Dolly shrieked. She leaned over so far, Irene had to reach out and pull her back into the boat. Dolly spun, pushing at Irene's arms. "I saw her! I saw my mom! She's down there, Mrs. Kent." Claire hadn't seen Dolly this upset. Her curls were bouncing wildly. She looked like she wanted to jump into the water herself—a very bad idea. "Her eyes . . . I don't think she could see me. Can't you get her out?"

"Not at the moment. We have to reach the island. From there, we'll make a plan."

Dolly sat back, looking like she was about to burst into tears.

Silence descended again, and Claire watched the wisps of people swirling below. There was a woman wearing overalls. A man in a long rain slicker. A teen boy wearing a high school letterman jacket. A girl in a long, billowy dress. They all passed by the canoe and then faded away into the depths. Claire was suddenly thankful that she had not seen the face of her father down there, staring blindly back up at her.

The flickering light among the trees on the darkening island was closer—brighter now, calling to her as if from another world.

Chapter Twenty-Three

A FEW MINUTES later, the canoes bumped up against the rocky bottom of the lake. The island's pines towered over them. Claire's chest felt tight as she helped drag the canoe up onto the shore. Her father's light was gone now. Had someone extinguished it? Or was it merely blocked by the trees? "Dad!" she called out, but Irene shushed her.

"Don't draw attention. We'll reach him on our own."

"But how? The light's gone."

Irene seemed to listen to something only she could hear. Then she headed toward the woods. "Follow me."

The night had come quickly, and as they moved

farther into the center of the small island, darkness surrounded them. Irene held one of the flashlights. Lucas directed the other. The pale spots lit bare branches. Above, an owl—or some great bird—let loose a fearsome hoot before flapping off in search of prey.

Claire wanted to call out to her father again. She wanted him to answer her, to come running through the pine saplings and gather her up in his strong arms. Instead, she pressed her lips together, breathed through her nose, and tried not to scream.

Beyond the reach of the flashlights, a separate glow appeared. Claire tensed. Her throat began to close as she choked back waves of emotion. From between two trees, a small blaze came into view. On the ground beside it was the body of a man.

Claire bolted forward, crashing through the brush until she reached the illuminated clearing. She skidded to her knees. The body was lying before her, unmoving. He almost looked like a pile of clothes. But she recognized her father's red windbreaker, his green corduroy pants, rolled twice at the hem, and his familiar Doc

Martens with thick rubber soles. She pressed her palms against one of his shoulders.

She couldn't tell if he was warm or not. For a moment, she worried that she hadn't reached him in time. But then he coughed. He shuddered and turned over, gazing up at her. Fear brought tears to his eyes. His mouth went slack, and he began to tremble. "Claire? Is that you?" He grabbed her and pulled her close, his body racked with sobs. She was shaking along with him. "How did you find me?"

"I can't believe it," she heard herself say. "I can't believe you're here."

He held her at arm's length, taking her in. "It feels like I haven't seen you in an eternity." Then he glanced over her shoulder, and Claire heard footsteps coming up behind her. He took in the others and Claire saw awareness filter through him. He hung his head. "I put you all in danger. I feel like such a fool." He sniffed, then rose to his feet, brushing himself off. Irene walked toward the fire. "Irene," he whispered. She opened her arms, and he collapsed into them. "Thank you," he said.

"It isn't me you should be thanking," she answered. She held her hand out to the kids. "Your daughter. My grandson. You remember Lucas?"

"Of c-course." The ghost hunter shivered, then smiled.

"Hi, Mr. Holiday," Lucas said with a small wave. He was wearing a strange grin that Claire knew must be keeping hidden all sorts of feelings.

"And this is Dolly Snedecker," Claire continued, pulling her new friend closer. "We wouldn't have made it here without her help."

Dolly nodded. "A pleasure to meet you, Mr. Holiday. My mom and I are big fans."

"Thank you, Dolly," he answered. "Hey, aren't you from the motel?"

"The one and only Lost Village. That's how I met Claire and Lucas. They showed up early today, looking for you."

"How did you get out here, Dad?" Claire asked. "And why didn't you come back?"

Miles released a long sigh. "That is some story to tell." He shook his head. "Where's Clementine?"

"Checked out of the motel last night," answered Dolly. "Said she was going back to your office. She seemed pretty freaked out."

Miles nodded. "Good, good. She had reason to be. Still has reason, I suppose."

"Because of Lemuel Hush?" Lucas asked.

"Well, yes. Of course. But what's worse than a vengeful ghost with a penchant for drowning anyone who gets close to the lake?" He glanced at them, his eyes sad and full of warning. "There's someone in this town who is very dangerous. Someone who is not a ghost. Someone who's very much alive."

A voice resounded from the shadows beyond the campfire's reach. "You talking about me, Mr. Holiday?"

Chapter Twenty-Four

A MAN EMERGED from the darkness.

Claire's brain skipped like a stone across water, trying to figure out why his voice sounded familiar. It wasn't Tanner. Wasn't anyone she'd seen on the streets of the town that day.

No, but she *had* seen him. Had heard his voice.

In her father's footage.

This was Reed, the mayor of Hush Falls Holler.

"You know the old adage," the man continued. "If you don't have anything nice to say, don't say anything at all." In the firelight, his face became clearer. His brow was furrowed, his eye sockets painted with shadow. A long khaki coat was draped over his shoulders. In his right hand, he clutched a wooden baseball bat. Its tip dragged across the ground as he took a step closer.

Miles moved in front of the group, his fists clenched at his sides.

"Mayor Winterson," said Dolly. "What are you doing out here?"

"I followed you, honey." Reed grinned. "Followed all of you. What a day you've had. Snooping around. Breaking into places. Stealing evidence."

"Is anyone going to tell us what's going on here?" Irene asked.

"Stay back," Miles shouted at Reed. "I'm warning you."

"Or what? You'll exorcise me?" The mayor shook his head, raising the baseball bat toward the group. "No, I think it's time for me to finish what I started. Though I must admit, I'm surprised that old Mr. Hush hasn't already done the job for me. He's usually so good at this sort of thing."

"It was you," Claire whispered. She wanted to rush

forward and kick him. "You were the one who found the camera. You're the one who brought it to the police station."

Miles nodded. "Reed attacked me a couple of days ago by the water's edge. I'd just caught incredible and frightening footage of Lemuel Hush at the lake. I remember turning to run. But then I saw the mayor step out from the woods. He was holding this bat. The next thing I knew I was on the ground. I have a vague memory of being dragged away. Of being in a rowboat. Reed left me here on the island."

"But why?" Lucas asked.

"No one in the Holler is going to vote for you again!" Dolly yelled.

Reed chuckled. "Cute, kid. This town is important to me. I've made that perfectly clear. And I have plans for it. Big plans. Plans that nobody will stop. We need visitors. Tourists. It's the only way to bring business back to this area. Money is imperative to my constituents."

"And to you," said Dolly. "You own like half the run-down buildings in Hush Falls Holler."

"I'm not going to argue." Reed shrugged. "What better way to get our name on the map than to have a famous ghost hunter disappear during a scouting mission for his show? I bet we could even get away with putting something like *The World's Most Haunted Town* right on our emblem. But also, if I had allowed Miles to continue doing what he was doing, poking around in places he shouldn't be poking in, hunting our legendary spirit and trying to send him away . . . No. We need Lemuel around these parts. He's the reason people will keep coming back."

"So you knocked my dad on the head," Claire said through gritted teeth. "You brought him out here?"

"In the past, I always just let old Lemuel do his thing. We have something of a pact, Lemuel and me. He's most efficient."

"In the past?" Lucas repeated. "You mean, you've done stuff like this before?"

Reed's grin grew thinner. "I'm not proud of it."

Dolly shivered. "Who . . . who else have you done it to?"

He sighed while thinking how to answer. "People

who threatened our way of life. Spirit-sensitive people. People who thought they knew better how to solve the town's problems."

"*Spirit-sensitive*," said Irene. "I knew there was a reason I didn't want you coming here, Lucas. Dangerous for people like us."

Dolly spoke up, her voice growing stronger. "My mother thought she could solve the town's problems. My mother had an idea about the graveyard watch. Removing the curse. *My mother . . .*"

Now Reed looked truly repentant. "I couldn't let Missy do that, honey. You have to understand."

Dolly swung her arms out at him. "You killed her! You killed my mom!"

"I did nothing of the sort," he replied, holding the bat before himself like a shield. "I merely made sure she was in the wrong place at the wrong time. At certain times of day, the water's edge can be a very dangerous place."

Dolly shrieked. She tried to dash forward, but Lucas held her back, knowing she'd only get hurt. "Let me go. *Let me go!*"

Reed sliced the bat through the air; it moved with a cutting sound. Then he pointed it at Dolly's face. "I realize now that I'll have to stick around here and wait for Lem to do what he's going to do to you. All of you. You're not leaving. You must know that."

Miles grunted. Then, before Claire could stop him, he rushed at the mayor, tackling him to the ground.

Chapter Twenty-Five

"RUN!" MILES CALLED out. He wrestled Reed for the baseball bat, the two of them rolling in the dirt near the fire. "All of you. Back toward the water."

Claire felt paralyzed. There was no way she was leaving him here. "Dad! No!"

"Go! Now!" Miles throttled Reed, forcing him onto his back. He sat on Reed's chest and then clasped the bat, yanking it from the mayor's hands. Miles raised it over his head threateningly.

Irene shuttled the three kids into the woods, shining the flashlight across the overgrown path. Claire kept trying to look back, to see if her father was okay. But Miles called out, "Go! Get away from here!"

The rocky beach appeared. Claire stepped on a stone, and her ankle bent at a strange angle. She fell to the ground and rolled to a stop. The others rushed to check on her. "I'm okay," she insisted. "But what about my dad? Did he follow us?" Lucas kept his flashlight pointed at the line of trees.

Seconds later, Miles appeared. He stumbled toward them, then collapsed beside Claire. Now it was his turn to rest his hands on her. "Are you okay, Clary?" he asked.

She nodded. "Where's the mayor?"

"He's not going to bother us anymore."

Claire wasn't sure what that meant, and she did not want to think about it. She forced herself to sit up. Rubbing at her ankle, she looked to the canoes. There was a rowboat pulled up onto the beach not far from where the group was huddled. The mayor's boat. "We should push his boat out into the water when we leave. So he can't come after us."

"Oh, I don't plan on following you." Reed barreled out of the woods toward the group. Lucas pointed his light at him, illuminating the red that was running down from a wound in his forehead. "Because none of you are leaving this place." Reed opened his jacket and pulled out the antique revolver that Claire had seen in a glass case at the Hush Falls Museum that afternoon. "I didn't want to have to do this. But you've forced my hand."

Claire felt ice shards pressing into her temples. It was a terror unlike anything she'd ever imagined.

"Stand up," said the mayor. The group did as he told them. "Drop the flashlights. Move back toward the water." They had no other choice.

Claire and Lucas stood behind her father. Irene moved in front of Dolly. Claire felt snot running over her top lip. Her father squeezed her hand, and a thought popped into her brain: We can be with Mom again. It won't be so bad. We can all be ghosts that haunt the Victorian house in Archer's Mills. People might even tell stories about us.

"Lemuel!" Reed called out over the water. "I brought you more of what you're looking for!" A loon called back with a maniacal hoot. "Lemuel Hush! Where are you hiding?"

Then another thought came to Claire: She could still protect them. The orb of white light! She focused on the image in her mind. She imagined her mother's wide arms surrounding her father and her friends, the warmth of her heart, the soothing sound of her voice, a sound that could erase all fear. *Help us, Mom. Help us.*

"You don't have to do this, Reed," said Irene calmly. "There are many ways to get what you want for this town. I can help you. We all can."

"My mom wanted to change things," said Dolly. "She wanted to free Mr. Hush. To protect the people of the Holler. If you'd really cared—"

"That was never going to happen. I couldn't risk sending Lemuel away. The World's Most Haunted Town needs to keep its most famous ghost!" The mayor's chest heaved, and he struggled for breath. He kept his focus on the group as he wandered down the beach and perched on the edge of his rowboat. The flashlights that Lucas and Irene had left behind were pointing toward him, casting him with an otherworldly glow. "I really am sorry," he told them. Then, frustrated, he threw his head back and shouted, "LEMUEL HUSH, WHERE ARE YOU?"

The rowboat jolted beneath him, somehow yanked several feet backward into the lake. Reed toppled off its side, falling facedown into the shallow water.

Claire paused in her meditation. Her breath hitched. She wanted to turn to the others and scream: *RUN*. But her father squeezed her hand even more tightly, keeping her still.

Reed lifted up his face from the water. He glanced around in confusion. Then the rowboat was ripped from the shore, disappearing out onto the dark water, too far for the flashlights to reach anymore. "Lemuel, no," Reed muttered, staggering up onto his hands and knees. "I'm not the one you want. I'm trying to *assist* you."

"No, he's not!" Dolly called out. "He's been sabotaging you, Mr. Hush! Reed Winterson is your enemy!"

But then a different kind of light became visible several feet from Reed, out on the water. A man rose up from the depths and hovered just above the surface. His fur collar was soaked through with lake water, holding it like a sponge. It dripped down his coat, splashing delicately into the lake. The soft sound defied the rage that was painted across Hush's face. His eyes filled with burning blue flame. "They're lying," Reed spat. "Lemuel, we're a team!"

"We're not lying," said Lucas. Lemuel glanced at the group. "You heard him yourself. He couldn't risk sending you away. He needs you, Mr. Hush. You do not need him!"

Reed swung the revolver toward the group. "You shut your mouths!" he shouted. In a flash, Lemuel was at the shore, his fingers grabbing at the mayor's neck. Wide-eyed, Reed rushed away from the water and bolted toward the group.

For a moment, Claire feared that he meant to snatch one of them up, put them in a headlock, hold them hostage. But his eyes were focused beyond them, at the woods. He was merely trying to escape. Claire stuck out her throbbing foot, catching the mayor by the ankle.

The man tumbled to the stony beach, the revolver flying out several yards in front of him.

Dolly did not hesitate. She scooped up the gun, then threw it out into the shallows, where it disappeared with a plop.

"Move!" said Miles, leading the group back toward the line of trees, leaving the mayor lying facedown on the shore. Claire looked over her shoulder to see Reed rise up onto his hands and knees. He groaned, then glanced at them with an anger that rivaled the look on Lemuel's face moments earlier. Lemuel was nowhere to be seen.

"Oh, no, you don't!" Reed was on his feet again. "Get back here!" he called to them. He turned toward the spot where Dolly had thrown the gun and then splashed toward it, dunking his hand under the surface as he scrambled to find it.

"Into the woods," said Irene. "Hurry."

"Wait!" Lucas whispered, planting his feet. "Look!"

A thick arm made of glowing blue light zipped up from the water just behind where Reed was crouched. Its ghostly hand clasped the bottom of the mayor's jacket and then ripped the man backward into the shallows. Reed reached toward the shore, bleating a brief cry before Lemuel Hush dragged him away from the island, out toward the depths, water filling his throat and stopping his voice.

The surface was frenzied for only a brief time.

After a while, it went still again.

Chapter Twenty-Six

AT THE EDGE of the woods, the group waited and watched. No one said anything for a long time—not even to ask if the others were okay. The answer to that didn't seem important at the moment.

Eventually, Claire spoke up. "We can't leave things like this."

Lucas examined her face. There was something about her eyes that looked hopeful and sad at the same time. "What do you mean?"

Claire looked to her father. "We should do what Dolly said earlier."

"What was it I said?"

"Your mother wanted to rid the town of the graveyard watch."

Dolly nodded with confusion. "She'd petitioned the mayor to dig up Mr. Hush's grave. Move his bones somewhere else. But in order to do that, we'd have to—"

"We'd have to reach the bottom of the lake," Lucas finished. His mind was whirling. He stared at his grandmother. She seemed suddenly goddess-like to him. More magical than he'd ever imagined. "You can do it, Gramma, can't you?" He glanced at Claire and knew that this was exactly what she'd been thinking.

"I can ask them to help us. The spirits who drowned here." Irene nodded at the dark water, where the mayor had gone under. She turned to the group. "But I'm going to need your assistance too. All of you. In several ways."

"Anything you need, Mrs. Kent," Claire answered. She tugged her father's hand and looked up at him with a sad smile. "Right, Dad?"

Miles simply nodded.

A few minutes later, with flashlights positioned toward the waterline, the group stood back and observed as Irene once more raised her hands. Her whispering rose up like the wind, like waves, like distant thunder approaching quickly. Lucas thought of his parents. Of their work. And he wondered how much someone like his gramma, or even someone like him, could make a difference along the coast.

Claire and Miles whispered to each other about the orb, using it to keep Mr. Hush at a distance.

The water began to churn, then to spin. It was just like it had been earlier that afternoon, when Gramma had rescued Tanner Worley. The surface dipped as the whirlpool widened. The spirits were listening to Gramma, helping her hold it wide. The mouth of the opening glowed blue, tendrils of color spiking around the hole, then retreating, then spiking again in a mesmerizing display. The portal moved, stopping a short distance from shore. Its watery walls dropped to the lake floor, so that if someone were to stand inside it, their feet would be pressed into the lake muck. The opening grew wider as the portal floor descended the slope, the walls stretching downward, extending a passageway deep into the lake. The rushing sounded just like the waves from Lucas's visions that day, when Lemuel had tried to scare him.

But now he didn't find the sound scary.

Instead, it filled him with wonder.

Standing at the tunnel's mouth, Lucas stared straight down into the depths of the reservoir. He imagined what he would find at the end of the watery passage, but there was no way to know until he made the journey down. "Is everybody ready?" he asked.

Irene took the lead. She continued whispering, talking to the spirits, asking them to part the water. Lucas and Dolly followed several feet back, directing the flashlights. Claire and Miles took the rear, still meditating on the protective light.

The tunnel felt like a cave—damp, dark, dangerous. It was strange to climb down this slope. Once upon a time, people had lived here. How long had it been since they had walked on this ground? Lucas glanced upward. The ceiling and walls of the tunnel looked like glass. Every few steps, there was another bluish flash along their surface that reminded him of where he was, of the magical thing that was happening, of what they were about to do.

Down and down they went. When the ground leveled off, there were patches of muck so thick, Lucas wasn't sure they would be able to continue on. But each of them managed to pull their feet up and out, taking only a few steps before struggling again and again.

Soon, something appeared in the water beyond the walls of the tunnel, a great structure that flashed when Lucas and Dolly moved their lights across it. Lucas knew what it was. He'd seen it in his nightmare last night. The old Hush homestead. Its tower tilted slightly. The line of its roof drooped like a Slinky toy. But the double doors stood shut, just as he had seen them. And if the doors were there, that must mean the graveyard was—

He turned to find the passage slithering out before him. He remembered the sounds he'd heard. *Tap. Tap. Tap.* But down here, it was quiet now. Claire and Miles's meditation must be working.

"I can't believe this," said Dolly. "I never imagined . . ." She shook away her amazement. "Which gravestone are we looking for?"

"It should be . . . this way."

Now the group was following him. He trod across limp lake weed until he reached one particularly large stone. He crouched and moved his hand across it, revealing the name engraved there.

Lemuel Hush.

And that was all. No epitaph. No dates. It was as simple as simple could be. As if the family had buried the man quickly and efficiently and then were done with him.

"How do we dig him up?" asked Dolly. "With our hands? That'll take all night."

Lucas shook his head. He peered to the left of the

stone, where a pair of rusted spades were half buried in the mire. He grabbed them both, then handed one to Dolly. "You have somewhere else to be?"

She smirked. They looked to the others, who were doing their own kind of work. Then they plunged the spades into the thick lake bottom.

Chapter Twenty-Seven

IT TOOK SOME time and lots of sweat, but Lucas and Dolly eventually dug down until they felt their spades clank against a solid surface.

The casket was made of wood. And the wood was thoroughly rotted. With a few hard whacks, they broke through the plank. Inside, soaking in the wet black depth of the grave, a skull stared up.

Dolly squealed and Lucas drew back. But only for a moment. Despite the nausea churning at the back of his throat, he knew there was still a lot of work to be done. He looked up and noticed Irene and Claire and Miles peering down at them. Each was soaking wet, covered with filth, their faces etched with shock and revulsion. Over their heads, another blue spike flashed, and Lucas took it as a sign to hurry up.

Dolly had already begun chipping away at the casket lid. He joined in. Soon, there was space enough to reach inside. But Lucas hesitated. What if bony fingers closed around his wrist? What if the rotting jaw chomped his fingers? Dolly didn't wait for him. She grabbed Lemuel's skull and yanked it from the coffin. She glanced at it briefly with disgust before tossing it up out of the dank hole. They worked together, removing bones, until the casket was empty, then they crawled out themselves.

Irene and Miles had already fashioned a type of satchel out of Miles's windbreaker. Miles stood shivering in a button-down shirt. The bundle sat on the ground between them, bulging with Lemuel's remains.

"Time to go?" Lucas asked his gramma. She nodded.

Together, the group dragged the bones across the muck, past the drowned mansion, toward the slope. Then they made their way up what had once been a hillside in the center of Hush Falls. And when they crawled out at the top, tumbling onto the stony beach, lying breathless, each of them stared up at the starry sky above them.

The portal collapsed with a crash so loud it made Lucas cringe and cover his head. Everyone sat up and looked out from the shore, where the water flickered and glimmered with light.

At first Lucas thought it was the rippling waves distorting a reflection of the stars, but then he realized it was the spirits, still lingering just below the surface.

"What now?" asked Claire.

"Are we safe?" asked Dolly.

"Look," said Lucas. He sat back, astonished. They followed his gaze.

The bluish lights were rising up, breaking through the lake. They no longer looked like the people they had once been. Now they gleamed—stretching and breaking, the way clouds change shape while moving across a summer sky.

Dolly stood, running close to the water's edge,

holding up her hands as if to catch rain. "Mama!" she called out. "It's me! It's your Dolly!"

"Careful, Dolly," said Claire.

But Dolly didn't care. "Mama! You're free!" A piece of the blue glimmer wafted toward her, almost touching Dolly's wiggling fingertips. She broke into wild laughter as her mother faded into the night.

"If the spirits are no longer trapped in the lake," Lucas said, glancing at the parcel filled with bones, "does that mean Lemuel is no longer here either? Did digging him up release his spirit too?"

"Listen," Irene answered.

Lucas shook his head. "What am I supposed to hear?"

"What *do* you hear?"

He thought for a moment. "Nothing."

Irene smiled. "Me neither. Lemuel Hush is no longer with us. He can't hurt anyone anymore."

"And neither can the mayor," said Claire. "Right, Dad?" She turned to where her father had been lying. But he was no longer there. She looked around. "Dad?"

she called out. Her voice echoed across the lake. "Did any of you see where he went?" She grabbed one of the flashlights and swung it around, sending its white spot across the small beach.

Lucas's stomach clenched. He glanced at his gramma. When he saw the look on her face, he understood. Staring at Claire, he felt a stinging in his nose. She continued to wave the flashlight, searching for her father.

Searching.

Searching.

Searching.

Chapter Twenty-Eight

THEY MADE IT safely back to the other side of the lake. Claire had ridden with Irene this time. She'd sat in stunned silence the entire way, staring straight ahead, as if looking into a different dimension.

She hadn't believed Lucas when he told her. He'd been caught up in the moment and hadn't realized the truth until Miles had suddenly vanished. When Irene confirmed it, Claire had shut down.

The man they had discovered out on the island had been her father's ghost.

They hadn't reached him in time.

No one knew why Miles hadn't looked like the

others, all bluish and transparent. Maybe, Lucas thought, it was because Miles hadn't known he'd been dead. Or maybe spirits appear differently to different people.

Though Lucas was more spirit-sensitive than ever before, he had no way of foreseeing what would happen in the next few hours: How Dolly's grandparents and father would come racing out of the motel office when Irene's truck pulled into the lot, how they'd scoop her up and hug her and then yell at her for running off, shout at all of them for taking their Dolly away. How quickly the police would arrive after Irene called them. The looks on their faces when Irene showed them what was inside the makeshift satchel. How many questions they would ask after Lucas told them his version of the story.

How Claire found it impossible to speak to them.

To him.

To anyone.

The next morning, the police scoured the island. They found Miles lying in the same spot that Claire had found him, next to an ash pit where he'd built himself a fire. After examining him, a doctor determined that the blow he'd received from the mayor's baseball bat had caused a slow bleed inside his head, and that after he'd fallen asleep beside the blaze, he did not wake up again.

Chapter Twenty-Nine

Dear Claire,

It's been a while now. I hope you're feeling better. I sure am. At least, I think I am.

Since you never wrote back a couple of months ago, I wanted to try again, to let you know that I'm still thinking about you.

I probably always will be.

Things are different here now. All those things that the mayor said he wanted to happen? Well—they're happening. After the news broke about what he'd done to your father, to my mother, to who knows how many others, people started showing up in Hush Falls Holler.

They want to see where it all happened. My grandparents' motel has been packed every weekend, but Gram and Gramps have been nice enough to let me keep my room to myself. They turn away paying customers! Just for me! I guess they *feel* bad about what I went through with you guys.

I *feel* bad about it too.

I don't care that the town is doing well now, or that there's talk about people wanting to start moving back to this area, or that we might even get a new library. I don't care about any of it. In fact, I asked my gram if we could leave. She said she'd think about it, but I bet she didn't really mean it. Not now that business is booming.

Claire, I wanted to ask you a question. What is it like to *feel* haunted? I mean, you would know, right? You're the ghost hunter's daughter, after all. There are some days when I think I can sense my mother nearby. Does that mean she's haunting me? Or does it mean that I'm just remembering her?

All I know is that I miss her. More than anything.

I bet you're feeling the same way about your parents. I'm sorry.

Do you know who else I miss? You and Lucas.

I was hoping that maybe one day I could come visit you in Archer's Mills. And I could bring my ghosts with me and introduce them to your ghosts and we could all have a nice tea party or something.

You probably think I'm a weirdo. But I don't care. You know who else people thought was weird? My namesake. Good ole Dolly Parton. And look what happened to her! She's totally famous, just like I plan on being one day.

winkety-wink

I'm so glad I have someone to write to. It's a lonely feeling putting words to paper and not having someone answer you. I used to do that all the time. Not so much anymore. Write me back, Claire, if you don't mind. You might find that it helps you too.

Your friend,

Dolly Snedecker

Chapter Thirty

ONE AFTERNOON NEAR the end of summer vacation, Lucas was lying on the couch reading a spooky book about some kids trapped in a haunted mansion, when he heard a knock at the door. His first instinct was to cringe, then shoot up to see who, or what, was there. But his gramma had been teaching him techniques that were allowing him to slow down, to notice his surroundings, to not let his brain jump to conclusions. So he took a deep breath. He stood, walked to the door, and without thinking whether or not it was one of his "visitors," he turned the knob. Claire stood on the front porch. She was turned slightly, gazing off into the distance, toward the breezy horizon where green trees swayed and danced. Her bike was propped up near the bottom of the steps. After a moment, she looked at him and smiled.

"Hi," she said.

"Hello. Everything okay?"

"Just thought I'd say . . . hi."

He grinned. "You did a very good job."

She chuckled. "Can I come in?"

It had been a difficult season. When he had first returned from the Holler, he hadn't spoken to Claire for a long time. He'd wanted to, but she wouldn't leave her house. And she hadn't wanted visitors—not even Clementine, her father's assistant, who'd tried several times since the trip to make contact. Claire's aunt, Lizzie, had become like a bodyguard, turning away friendly phone calls as well as requests for interviews, keeping gawkers off their front lawn, and shouting at people who walked by the red Victorian just a little too slowly. He'd kept his distance.

He didn't blame Claire for wanting to keep to herself. He couldn't imagine what she was feeling.

Besides, he was struggling with his own stuff.

Everything that had happened on their trip had felt like a dream. And still, there were nights when the dream continued. Lemuel Hush would show up when Lucas was on the edge of sleep and grab at him. Even in his most ordinary dreams, waves would suddenly rise from nowhere and wash everything away.

Gramma had explained that there were different kinds of dreams. Sometimes spirits used them for communication. But most times, they were just our brains trying to process our lives, our fears, our disappointments, our joys.

He often wondered what Claire's dreams were like now. And Dolly's, for that matter.

Dolly had written him several kind letters. And he had surprised himself by writing her back. He liked Dolly. Despite everything she had been through, she managed to seem upbeat. Happy. It was like her skin was bulletproof. It was admirable. He was still trying to work up the courage to ask her how she did it. Maybe it was all that Dolly Parton music. He'd promised himself he would give her a listen sometime soon.

After school ended for the year, his parents had come to visit. It was awkward at first, since he hadn't seen them in such a long time, and he had so much to talk to them about, but they eventually settled into a family routine for the duration of their stay. Breakfast. Walks around the neighborhood. Even folding laundry together was fun. He hadn't felt that safe in a long time. And when they had to go back to the coast, it took several days for him to wake up in the mornings and not feel afraid that he'd never see them again.

Halfway through that summer, Claire had shown up at his house. She'd apologized for being invisible lately. He'd hugged her. They sat on the steps quietly and just listened to the wind. Then she said she had to go.

Next time, she stayed a little longer.

The time after that, she actually stepped inside Gramma's house, sat on the couch, and watched some television.

Soon, Claire was visiting regularly. She liked to ask him about his gift—about hearing the knocking. She wanted to know how it worked, what he felt, what he saw. He did his best to explain, though he was still trying to figure it out himself.

One morning, after he'd heard a knocking and had answered the door, he'd shown up at Claire's house and asked if she wanted to join him in delivering a *message*. She'd smiled, her eyes going wide with excitement, and said, "I thought you'd never ask."

Now, they went back to the kitchen. He took two cans of Coca-Cola from the fridge, and they sat on the high stools at the center island, cracking open their drinks and swigging deeply.

"I wanted to ask you a question." Claire placed her can down on the counter. It clinked softly.

"Shoot," he said.

"I understand that your visitors come to you. They're the ones who knock."

Lucas nodded patiently. They'd been over this several times.

"But I was wondering if it could work the other way around. Like, can *we* knock too?"

Lucas sighed. "Well, isn't that what your father used to do on his show? He'd reach out to the other side. Make them answer?"

"I don't like how my father did it. Irritating the spirits so they'd respond. It never felt right to me. I was wondering if you knew a different way?"

"I can ask my gramma."

Claire shrugged. "I just thought, if there was something simple that you knew of . . . something I could do myself, whenever I was feeling, you know, alone." She was quiet for a long time. "I was hoping . . . even though I'm not special like you and Mrs. Kent . . . that I might find a way to talk to them again. My parents."

Lucas didn't have an answer. He took another sip of his cola. The bubbles burned, then tickled the back of his throat. Something came to him. Something he was pretty sure would work. "You could always just . . . *talk* to them. You don't need any special training to do that. Do you?"

Claire's expression fell. It wasn't what she'd wanted to hear.

"I'm still waiting for them to visit me," he said. "I'm sure they will sooner or later."

She stood. Her smile was worn, showing the sadness hiding underneath. "I'm sure they will too," she answered. He didn't need to be psychic to know she didn't mean it.

Lucas walked her back outside. Claire lifted her bike from the porch steps. "Are you excited for school to start up again?"

She sniffed, then rolled her eyes. "I already spent half the summer making up what I missed after our trip. I think I need a longer break."

"Keep wishing." He laughed.

"I will." She swung her leg up over the crossbar, then settled onto the bike seat. "See you later, Lucas."

"See you."

She waved goodbye, then turned and glided off down the long driveway.

Epilogue

From Claire Holiday's
personal video journal

[Image—Claire appears on
screen. Leans back in her desk
chair. Her bedroom comes into
focus behind her. She smiles.]

Claire—Hi, Mom. Hi, Dad.

I'm putting your camera to
good use again, Dad. You'd be
proud.

Just wanted to check in with
you guys. Give you an update.

School's going well, I
guess. I got a B on that math
test, which Aunt Lizzie says is
great, but I'm not so sure. I
thought I studied harder than
for just another B!

Lucas says hi. He's still
waiting for you to come
knocking. So am I. But I guess
for now, this is good enough.
[pauses] His gramma Irene says
that maybe you're not knocking
because you haven't stuck
around. Like, you don't have
any "unfinished business" here
on earth . . . which made me
slightly angry because . . .
Hello! [points her fingers at
herself] I am your "unfinished
business." [laughs] But I guess
if I think about it, it's a

nice thing. A good thing.

Because that means you're both

happy where you are. And I . . .

feel better knowing that.

I mean, I miss you so much.

But . . . Lucas was right. It's

so easy to reach out to you.

And I'm pretty certain that

you're listening. So thanks

for that.

I only wish . . . I wish you

would send me a little sign.

Like Mom did with the stars

that night. It doesn't have to

be much. A touch on the cheek.

Finding my book bag on my desk

chair in the morning after I

left it on the floor. A

sputtering candle would make

me happy, especially on the

nights when my feelings come

like giant waves. I never
thought I'd say this, but I'd
love to sense that you are
watching. Do you think you can
make that happen?

[pause, eyes skyward] I
guess if I think about it,
maybe things like this have
already happened.

In fact, I'm pretty sure
they have. I'm sorry.

I'll pay closer attention
from now on.

Okay, that's all for now. I
have to get up early for
school, but what else is new? I
miss you. I love you. But what
keeps me going and gets me
through the times that feel
sticky and rough is knowing
that you loved me too, and you

love me still, forever and for
always.

Good night.

[Claire kisses at the camera
lens. She reaches toward it.
Flips a switch.]

[The screen goes black.]

Acknowledgments

I would first like to thank the teachers, librarians, and parents who understand why scary stories can be important for young people and who make sure they end up in the right hands.

Thank you to Nick Eliopulos for signing up this spooky baby. Special thanks to Erin Black for adopting her when she was orphaned and for allowing me the time and space and encouragement to allow her to grow. I'd also like to thank Keirsten Geise, Josh Berlowitz, Jessica White, Courtney Vincento, Taylan Salvati, David Levithan, and every other wonderful person on the Scholastic team for all their brilliant work.

My agent, Barry Goldblatt, talked me through some difficult moments, spurring me to finish this story when I wasn't sure I could.

Matthew Sawicki listened to me read bits and pieces of this manuscript and enthused along the way.

Thank you to my mother, Gail, and my stepfather, Bruce, for bringing me up to Quabbin Reservoir in Massachusetts for some historic inspiration.

Thanks to Amanda and Anthony at *Rough Draft* in Kingston, NY, for allowing me to be part of their creative community. Thanks also to the folks at *Writers Speak Easy*, especially Matt Clegg, who listened to some early chapters and helped me make them even creepier.

As always, thank you to my friends and my family.

And most of all, thanks to all of you for reading my books over these years. I appreciate you more than you know.

About the Author

Dan Poblocki is the author of many books for young people, including *The Ghost of Graylock*, *The Haunting of Gabriel Ashe*, *The House on Stone's Throw Island*, *The Book of Bad Things*, and the Shadow House series. His stories have thrilled and chilled readers all over the world. In the US, they have won several state reading awards, have been named to the Best Books for Young Adults list by the American Library Association, and have been honored by the Junior Library Guild. Dan lives in Saugerties, New York, in an old house where he tries very hard to ignore the things that go bump in the night.

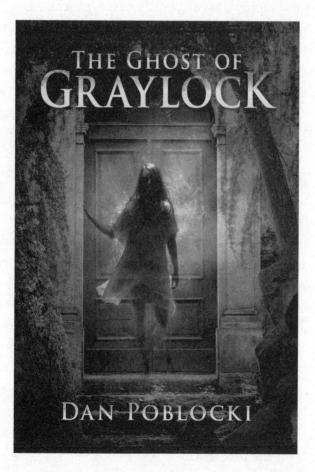

EVERY TOWN HAS its share of secrets. And when whispered by children in the dead of night, some secrets become stories. Sometimes, under special circumstances, the stories become legends, destined to survive even as the children who share them grow up and move on.

In a town called Hedston, a ruined building called Graylock Hall stood in the state forest like an enormous funeral monument. It had once been a notorious psychiatric hospital housing almost one thousand patients. Local kids referred to it as "the asylum in the woods," and most of them knew well enough to stay away. Since its closing, the secrets contained within the hospital's walls had given rise to a frightening legend of madness and murder. If you'd grown up nearby, the subject of that legend—a nurse who had worked the graveyard shift—would have haunted your nightmares from an early age.

It started with a storm.

Late one night while the hospital was still in operation, the building lost electricity during a thunderstorm. In the blackout, one of the patients from the youth ward went missing. The next morning, the staff found the girl's body—drowned, bloated, and blue—facedown in the reeds at the water's edge.

Then, several months later, a second patient drowned—another storm, another power outage. Some of Graylock's staff grew suspicious of the nurse who had been on duty during both accidents, but they said nothing. After a third drowning, the staff wished they hadn't kept their fears secret.

Three children lost. Three bodies discovered at the water's edge—small limbs tangled in lake weed, eyes staring blindly at the pale morning sky.

The people of Hedston refused to believe that the deaths were a coincidence. And so they arrested the nurse who'd worked the graveyard shift, claiming that the madness of the place had infected her—that she had decided death was the only way to end the suffering of the children in her charge. To add to the townspeople's horror, a day after her arrest, the police discovered the nurse's body hanging from a bedsheet that she'd tied to the bars of her cell.

With the nurse's death, the truth would remain her secret, a secret that became a story, a story that became a legend.

Within a few short years, the hospital was shut down. Graylock Hall was left to rot, but in the town of Hedston, the tale of Nurse Janet lived on.

And they say that, inside the abandoned building, a woman in white still wanders the corridors, her thick-heeled shoes click-clacking against the tile as she follows at an arm's length behind anyone who dares intrude. When she catches you, she sticks you with her needle, then drags you outside to the water's edge, down to the deep tangles of clutching lake weed.

They say she smiles as she holds you under—her face blurred as you stare up through the silvery surface, her teeth glistening white—delighted to continue her murderous quest to end the suffering of the insane. For who but those with their own touch of madness would dare enter the asylum in the woods and pursue its terrible secrets?

Everyone knows you'd have to be crazy to do something like that.

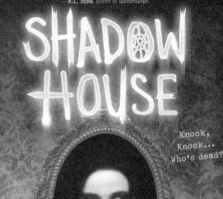